DOX

◆

DOX

a novel by Alex Beaumais

published by *tragickal*
cover & typesetting by *tragickal*
edited by Ilario Meyer
first edition

the only question is whether you blame yourself

www.tragickal.com
ISBN 9798574882368

in tyrannos

Table of Contents

Alex Beaumais

tragickal

| Prologue |

Ron Ogórek tiptoed away from his daughter once her eyes were fixed to the TV screen. The calm that came over her when she stared into LED was so intense that he was sure in that state Jane could learn differential equations or ancient Chinese; yet mostly she watched *Arthur* reruns and YouTube videos about historical fires. (Currently, a documentary about the Chicago fire of 1871.) Sometimes he thought he was a bad father for letting a fire fixation fester in her, but nothing soothed her like holding a screen and staring into flames.

Through the kitchen window, the setting sun bulged like a mango in a fizzy jar. Ron went through the basement door, his shin splints slowing him on the steps down to the wine rack—wine as a hail mary after huffing on a paper bag and watching his favourite *Genghis Khan* episode. He wanted to sit under the stars, zooming in (if he could remember how) on Canis Major with the telescope his middle daughter, Bela, had given him. On the bottom step his left arm throbbed like he'd hurled a piano over the roof. He kicked open the cellar door, wedged it with a brick. As he reached into the rack for his last bottle of u-brew Jutrzenka, a flurry of pinpricks tickled his chest with dark pleasure. He inhaled: one, two. Had he drunk too much at dinner again, or not enough? His daughters had turned on each other at the dinner table, the stupid girls had almost murdered each other over some kraut, a *głupi niemiec* boyfriend. He didn't know if he'd get outside with the telescope. Maybe he would just go to bed and be nice to himself.

Through the basement window, a crescent moon shone like a watermark in the sky. Wondering if it was a bad omen to see the sun and moon so close, he turned around and his foot smashed the brick, sending it to the wall. The door slammed. The bottle detonated on the concrete and lightning shot through his heart. He writhed on the floor, chewing his tongue among the shards, thinking about bad omens.

| Making Friends |

Ariel idled in her new-car-smelling Kia, wondering if, as a feminist, she'd made the right decision. She'd decided against the Honda Civic and Mazda3 as too bourgeois, too fratboyish. She'd felt "respectable" in the Ford Fusion, but didn't trust this quality—a dog-whistle of structural violence—plus there was Henry Ford's antisemitism. She'd considered the Chevrolet Malibu in solidarity with Labour, but the thought of her Coors-guzzling, buck-shooting cousins in Michigan had quashed that. Questions of practicality had kept her from a Tesla much less than an association with tech bros. As she'd planned a second test drive of the Toyota Prius Hybrid, the Kia dealership had called to slash the price by $1400 and throw in a year of oil changes. So here she was, waiting in the humming Rondo for her sister Bela, and she'd claim poverty and ignorance if anyone raised objections to her choice of car.

Idling behind a fleet of taxis, Ariel stared down the dusty, mirage-wet street towards the crescent-topped Bloor Tower. She wondered which of Bela's friends would want to live in such a market-slaughtering condo—probably all of them—and which would have the money—probably none. But then again, Ariel could hardly name a single one of Bela's friends.

Ariel spotted her sister coming out the automated doors. Bela had a springy step, as though her heels were outfitted with hover pads. As Bela neared, Ariel saw the creases in her cheetah-print dress, saw the swollen purple of her eye contours. Once a year, Ariel appropriated this look through $40 of Sephora, but Bela achieved it on the regular.

Bela got in, her dress hiking almost to her thighs, and Ariel counted the seconds before Bela closed her legs. She put on her left-turn signal and looked for an opening in the traffic.

"Who lives in Bloor Tower?"

"Jerry. My friend.

"Just a friend?"

"Yeah, but…"

"But what?"

"Nothing."

Ariel looked over her shoulder and throttled into the traffic, overtaking a Dodge Ram whose driver blared his horn behind tinted windows. *Fuck!* If there was an accurate dictionary entry for "patriarch (n.)," then the cowboy in his tinted space-truck would be it. Ariel decided against venting

dox

these thoughts to her sister, because Bela tended to look for an exit when Ariel started expounding on social issues, and Ariel didn't need her walking into oncoming traffic—the family had enough issues. She also didn't want to look down too much on Bela, for whenever Ariel made her monthly visit to her father and two sisters, her general competency and aptitude, of which she had a ceaselessly fluctuating view, was thrown into generous relief.

They slowed to a red and Ariel said, "How do you know Jerry?"

"His cousin owns The Rubik's Cube, on Queen West. He pays me sometimes to hang around there. I mean, to hang out at the tables with bottle service."

"Are you sleeping with him? You can tell me."

"No. He gives me money and he gets nothing in return."

Ariel smiled at the not-fucking and at Bela's cute conception of this supposedly zero-sum exchange. If someone in her graduate seminar was asking, she was against her sister trading on and perpetuating trad-femininity for a bit of coin, which only strengthened the nexus between money and male sexual power. But she was well practiced in the woker position: that Bela should make money however the fuck she wants.

Ariel pulled onto Jarvis Street and tried to think of some remark to defuse the tension, or what she would describe to her therapist as tension. Before she could think of something, Bela said, "I have a date tonight."

Ariel didn't know what to make of this.

Bela said, "He's coming to the house for dinner."

"You have a date? That's so old-fashioned."

"Well, I did meet him online."

a. beaumais

"Where? OkCupid? Plenty of Fish?"

"SeekingArrangement."

When Ariel finally swallowed, she was unsure whether her feeling of alarm was alloyed with a grain of admiration—whether her sister was more a sultan's concubine or Miley Cyrus.

"Do you get worried that all sorts of weird men on there are going to recognize you on the street?"

"I don't show my face in my pictures."

"That's good," said Ariel. "I mean, you do you. It's good that you don't show your face if you don't want to. But if you did show your face, that'd be OK too because no one owns—"

"Yeah, OK," said Bela.

"Whatever!" snapped Ariel, one-upping her. As she drove, she thought of a paper she'd written during her M.A. degree, "Three Simulacra of Sexual Traumas and Cultural Signalling," which made use of Bela's stints as a webcam model who'd fallen into this type of sex work by accident, after witnessing, alongside a friend on Chatroulette one tipsy Friday, how the flash of a nipple, or the potential for one, could make men on the Internet part with their money. Ariel'd then gotten permission to watch Bela on Chaturbate as Bela chatted, fully clothed, with anonymous men in free chat and waited for one of her "regulars"—those who paid for items on her Amazon wish list—to message her for a session. When one did, Ariel had slipped off downstairs to start her essay, adding the cryptic conjecture (unbeknownst to Bela at that time, and still unknown, as Bela didn't read Ariel's blogs) that Bela's life had been altered by an Oedipal trauma related to their parents.

"Why'd you start using SeekingArrangement?" Ariel asked.

"I need to help more with the bills, now that dad's at home all the time. And this puts me in a better position."

"As a woman?"

"I guess. I don't know. I'm done with the webcam. And I'm deleting all my online dating profiles."

"Why?"

"Well, Rick doesn't like it. And I can see why–"

"What the *fuck*? You're letting some john you met on the Internet control your body?"

"He's not a john. He's actually really successful in the media."

"What? What media?"

"I don't know. You can ask him tonight, if you come to the house."

As she drove, Ariel fought her overeager expression, which she imagined as like a Rottweiler sniffing a half-opened can of Chef Boyardee. Although she was seldom jealous of her sister, save for her looks (notwithstanding their problematic alignment with cishet norms) and—once in a while—her gall, she did admire Bela's ability to maintain a blunt affect in the face of stimulating news—or maybe it was just that Bela didn't really give a damn about anything, which was out of reach for Ariel in a world of gross inequality, rising sea levels, and Donald Trump.

Bela passed her a $20 bill for gas and Ariel imagined its sweaty provenance in the back pocket of "Jerry," if that was really his name. Her eyes followed a contrail in the horizon as she tried to remember what it was she wanted to say. She called up the keywords in her mental cloud—

income inequality, rising sea levels, Trump, Jerry, ass sweat, infantilizing commodification, the Simulacra of Sexual Traumas and Cultural Signalling—but whatever it was flew over her head like the jet in the sky. Her foot lifted from the gas as her eyes retraced the arc of the contrail.

"Ariel!"

She swerved back into her lane as the Jeep behind them blared its horn.

"Camille Paglia!" said Ariel.

"What?"

"I just remembered: Are you still coming to my talk tonight on Camille Paglia and crypto-fascism?"

"Rick and I are going to a show. Assuming you get me home alive."

Ariel bore her teeth simian-like, raked over the coals by this insult burning with the embers of family absenteeism— her guilt that she didn't come around the house much. She gave the stink-eye to a blonde woman in the Jeep in her rear-view, remembering how Bela had promised—or at least said—she'd come to the talk. But Bela and the stupid blonde had rebuked her driving; she'd lost leverage. She drove on, her face a sullen mask of guilt and passive aggressiveness, hoping her silence would replenish some capital. She often worried that she ignored Jane, their youngest sister, the way Bela ignored her. But, on the other hand, she'd raised awareness of the autism spectrum through her highly trafficked *Buzzfeed* features, and what had Bela ever done for any cause?

Ariel drove faster, feeling the scales tip slightly in her favour. She relaxed: she had to let herself. She drew Deepak Chopra ohms into her diaphragm, topping up her authority over Bela—who, far from being qualified to bitch about her driving, lacked even a beginner's permit—the two of them waiting as a sirening ambulance wove and sped in fits through an intersection. As they let it pass, Ariel saw that the blonde in the Jeep was actually a woman in a hijab.

Ariel was relieved, as they waited for the cars to start moving, when Bela broke the silence by saying, "We need to do something about the Pomeranian."

But at this name, Ariel's heart blipped. This was her father's neighbour, "the Pomeranian"—whose pigfucker misanthropy had been debated and soliloquized for hours on end by the Ogóreks, with nothing to show for but palsied vocal cords. He was, in short, a bastard. There was nothing to suggest he was Pomeranian, or even Polish, except a vaguely Teutonized Slavic surname, but the moniker had stuck around to add to the legend.

"Have the police been involved?" asked Ariel.

"No, but he's claiming he owns a strip of our front lawn. And he's been cutting it. Just a metre across the length of it!"

"But it's on the other side of his driveway. What good is it to him?"

"He showed dad this land survey. And then dad showed him ours, which shows something different. And the Pomeranian keeps cutting the strip."

"Did you do anything about it?" asked Ariel.

"Last time he was cutting the strip, I went out there with dad and we asked him to stop. And he ignored us and we asked him again and he went inside and brought out the survey. I thought dad was going to murder him."

"Maybe he should," said Ariel.

Bela smiled. "I've been going out there and cutting

the rest of our lawn afterwards so daddy doesn't notice."

"That's treating the symptom, not the cause. Let's go there right now."

Ariel drove over the valley of gnarled trees under Sherbourne bridge and into Rosedale, downshifting upon the budding helicopter leaves, the bumble bees sprung from their pangs, a bandanaed woman sponging soap from a bucket and massaging her SUV. Ariel's visits to her father and two sisters in the trellised, redbrick, lopsided house had grown more sporadic, and she needed to make a bigger effort, needed to do better. But here she was now: it counted for something.

She parked behind the old shell of a station wagon, which was rusted like a caboose. The oversized family house, mortgaged recently to help pay down debt (including Ariel's grad school), was to Ariel a symbol of The Fall: the lie of Ron's bourgeois largesse, his belt no longer containing his gut. Despite her memories here, she would've rather pulled into a small duplex in a noisy Filipino or Tamil enclave, although she knew Jane needed space to destroy.

Bela started to the front door and when she examined her flower box of lemongrass and lavender—at least Bela'd achieved that—Ariel said, "Where are you going? We have business to attend to."

"Can't I pee first?" asked Bela, squatting in pulses, her hand ironing down her dress.

"Let's get this over with."

"At least let me change out of this."

"What does it matter what you're wearing?"

Bela followed her sister's orders and they walked down the driveway, Ariel snickering at the bolt of short weedy Ogórek lawn now nationalized by the Pomeranian.

They reached the sidewalk, went left, and turned left again up the Pomeranian's brick pathway, towards the snot-yellow house, the sight of which always injected a little infectious agent into whatever state Ariel was in. On the left half of the Pomeranian's front lawn was a thick-trunked, Y-shaped ash tree with a little door under the fork.

Almost two decades ago, at Bela's fifth birthday, when the legion of party girls were hoola-hooping on the front lawn, Ariel'd led the girls to the Pomeranian's to open the tree door and discover what was inside—a baby? an elf? a birthday cake? As they acted out stereotypically feminine girl roles, the Pomeranian had run outside in an apron and with a butcher's knife (there was a bit of uncertainty over this), gnashing his teeth, at least according to her memory (which was accurate in *spirit*, in his posture towards the world), and shooed the girls away. Ariel still didn't know what was behind the door in the tree.

On the stoop, under austere, human-length shrubs, Ariel reached her hand out to the doorbell.

"Wait!" Bela said.

"What now?"

"I don't want to deal with this now. Please. I'm not prepared. Can we do this later?"

"I can't believe you right–"

"He's not who you think he is," said Bela. "This is not going to end well."

"Just stand there and look pretty," said Ariel, ringing the doorbell. She was incredulous at this damsel-in-distress performance (although it was admittedly a bit funny, her sister wearing the cheetah-print dress). She heard footsteps inside, but didn't flinch. What could she be afraid of? She regularly brunched with former Toronto MP Cheri Dinovo and had been in a polycule with the daughter of a U of T provost. She had 8,000 followers on Twitter, including ANTIFA functionaries and hackers from SF to Berlin who'd cream themselves to put a white, heteronormative, patriarchal creep in their scopes. She patted the bulge of Mace Triple Action pepper spray—which she'd smuggled in with Shahzad on a cross-border trip to Port Huron and *always* kept in her pocket—the wind of the zeitgeist at her back.

A veiny hand opened the door half-way.

The Pomeranian squinted like a night-watchman shining a flashlight on peasants.

Slowly, Ariel ascertained that he wasn't going to speak or open the door. She said, "Hello sir, we live next door—I mean, my sister here does. We're the Ogóreks? May we have a word with you?"

The Pomeranian grunted in a way that was affirmative but showed his burnt wick.

He averted his icy, purple-ringed eyes from Bela and gawked at Ariel like a paper-skinned monster. Ariel said, "We understand there's been a little altercation over the subsection of our lawn adjacent your driveway. And I want to tell you personally that I recognize your right to your own claim, your own semantics, and I want to strive to avoid any failure of language here. But practically speaking, because we should be pragmatists, unless you want to enlarge your driveway, which is already somewhat sizeable, then we ask, neighbour to neighbour, that you give up the claim and accept our gratitude…"

The Pomeranian turned away, the leg of his corduroy overalls stained with oil or ink. He disappeared somewhere, maybe to the next room. Before Ariel could appraise the expression on Bela's face, the Pomeranian was coming at them through the door, carrying a folded map. Ariel hadn't seen him in at least five years, and yet he looked identical, as though at some point his features had been cryogenically frozen in place: his meaty, lopsided ears and orkish nose, his full head of Siberian-white hair, his cotton-stretching potbelly, the serpentine eyes behind horn rims.

"Look here," he said, unfolding a paper. He traced his stubby finger along the property border, which stretched past the sewer drain on the street (marked "SD") to encompass some of the Ogóreks' driveway. "It goes past the drain." He pointed and they looked behind them at the current de facto border—the edge separating the Ogóreks' lawn and the Pomeranian's driveway—which aligned with the middle of the sewer drain.

"Be that as it may," said Ariel, "practically speaking there's little benefit to you unless you want to expand your driveway. Also, we have our own map, which shows the boundary to be in line with the current norms."

"Your survey is from 1974. I've seen it," he said, pointing to a little crown and signature beside the legend.

"Be that as it may—"

"You—"

"Please don't interrupt me when I'm speaking."

"You have no legs to stand on, girls."

"Excuse me? Sorry, I'm going to let that go in the interests of cooperation here. Do you intend to pave over this strip you keep cutting?"

"Maybe. That's for me to decide."

"Sir," she said, arresting her vocal tear, "it would

benefit all parties in this community if we could reach a short-term agreement to be revisited later. I have experience in these kinds of mediations. Maybe we could mow your front lawn for a month as a gesture of goodwill. Bela, give him your phone number."

Bela ruffled through her purse, excavating her Galaxy as the Pomeranian shook his head, hissing "no, no, no." He licked his lips and stared at Bela as she held the blinking LED. "No battery," she said.

"I don't need the number." He closed the door a few degrees.

"Excuse me! See this line?" said Ariel, pointing back without looking. "This is not the Oder-Niessa line. Excuse me for being curt, but we are not provinces in the Soviet Union. You do not get to annex our property!"

The Pomeranian's eyebrows formed a bushy arch over his reptile pupils. He tremored, his fingers flushing pig-red as they gripped the door.

"I don't understand you!" he blared, like someone hard of hearing. "Why are you still here? Go on!"

"That's *exactly* what men like you always say! 'I can't understand you.' Always—"

"Get off my doorstep!"

The door flew in Ariel's face, fanning it with heat. The deadbolt clicked: "Always telling women and people of colour, 'I don't understand you. You are *so* mysterious! I am unable to fathom your exotic and inscrutable viewpoints and desires, so I'll pretend I didn't hear them!'"

Ariel turned to see her sister turning 90 degrees on the sidewalk. Ariel was throttled like a hummingbird as she left the Pomeranian's stoop and walked across his lawn and driveway, almost beating Bela to their door. Anger ejaculated through her ribs, eviscerating the detritus of her bourgeois, academic day writing PPT slides. She was *addicted* to the feeling of scaring herself—of summoning that Mesolithic feeling of shame that came from subverting hierarchies and town elders, of trolling white men.

Bela unlocked the front door and Ariel followed her, whiffing the woody musk of the foyer, dozens of shoes stacked like egg cartons. A bouquet of dandelions and forsythia soaked up dirt-flecked water in a square vase on the windowsill. Ariel wondered if Jane was home, but she didn't see her pink Reeboks on the Welcome. She'd heard how last Wednesday the Pomeranian had threatened to call the police after seeing Jane screaming in tears on the front lawn in a kimono and zori sandals, her skin powdered white and hair tied with a tortoiseshell kanzashi. Ariel had meant to tell him to be more tolerant and understanding. She almost wanted to go back now.

In the tearoom Ariel dropped down in the rocking chair, its limbs squealing a little more under her weight than she remembered. She was sure no one ever came in here, which had remained undisturbed since their mother left them nine years ago: the teak China cabinet, Bubble Boy painting, Singer sewing machine. The sun had bleached the quilt at the window and the grandfather clock was frozen at 9. Ariel sometimes wanted to enter with a garbage bag and purge the room of its memories, but stopped herself because she didn't know how Jane would react. As Ariel tapped out a badly auto-corrected text message to Shahzad, her boyfriend, telling him to come for dinner, Bela entered in her sweatpants.

"Can I use your phone?" she asked.

a. beaumais

"What happened to yours?"

"I forgot the charger at Jerry's."

She handed over her iPhone. When Bela left, Ariel read the text she'd written, which gave their address and to "come in 45." She wondered about Rick's media connections, whether he had cache in New York; whether he could open doors. She'd never met any of Bela's boyfriends, except James, who was older, but they were not to speak of him anymore because he was too much of a case for Bela's head.

A lid crashed on the kitchen floor, spinning out of control till it suddenly stopped.

"Do you need help in there?" called out Ariel.

"No," said Bela, and she was relieved.

Ariel righted her posture, straightening her back against the old oak and sliding her hands along the sloping arms. Closing her eyes, she funnelled air through her lungs and, when she was full and had conjured a sparkling, cathedral-sized Vishnu over a calm bay of tropical water, she exhaled through her nose, inwardly chanting "ohm" as the air stream fluttered the first arm of Vishnu—a gay mocha Buddha—like a wind chime. She drew breath again and swooshed the air toward the next arm—a non-conforming turbaned immortal cyborg—till the air fluttered the arm. And then she redirected the stream to a Hasidic boy on hormone replacement therapy, the smell of *bigaos* filling the tearoom, the western sun glimmering through the skylight, pinkening her closed-eye vision and warming her neck. The sunlight twirled on her face, jumping it like a battery. In her vision, below the levitating Vishnu from whom all creation stemmed, a golden urn leaked vespers over the water, which made her think of her disappeared mother, for some reason. She examined the next arm on her holy wheel and redirected her breath towards it, an asexual Kyoto herbivore man dressed for a Dragon Ball fair. As she alighted upon an Uppsala woman whose blond braids hid behind a niqab but whose aquamarine eyes were immodestly bright, the smell of pork crockets wafted like a street smell through her sensorium. She saw herself enshrouded last month at the #hijabweek solidarity drive organized by Cell #282. The smell of crochets was like a fart and her thoughts unspooled into BDS, the petrodollar, Muslim female modesty. She took a breath. She refocused her vision on the next arm of Vishnu: a dark, green-eyed Semitic girl in the holy land, burning in the pyre of history. Ariel's ohm echoed under the cliffs and through the tropical bay as she aligned her breath with the little girl's: same blood, same fears, same clock. As Ariel fused in oneness with the girl-bodied child, the appalling stooped silhouette of a Wojak flickered in the sky like a hologram. She tried to ignore it— Bela's new boyfriend—but the specter lurched over, speeding her heart rate, sending pulse waves of dread down her spine. Ariel said her mantra louder, defiantly embedding herself in the girl's green irises, which reflected the water: a dark purple convexity swelling, churning the surface, a scaley limb rising, currents pooling below, the tentacle soaring in the sky, a twin-headed serpent with two dozen eyes, a terrible island rising in the water.

Ariel tried to banish the omen, but the octopus tentacles took their grip, gnashing jaws, leviathan skull. She opened her eyes and reverted to a low-energy meditation, focusing only on her breath, which gradually overcame the tightness of her chest and the violence of her third eye. She restored calm and fell asleep in the afternoon sun.

a. beaumais

*

"He's here!"

Ariel opened an eye, wrenched from the REM-puzzle of sleep as if waking on the subway in her underwear. She hurried to the window, the essay sub-heading "Means of Reproduction" unreconciled with the under-ripe banana taste on her tongue. A gun-metal grey BMW sat in the driveway. A tall white man with black hair cut close at the sides and gelled in a flop on top passed the window in chinos, Birkenstocks, and a navy button-down. His silver Rolex relayed the sun into Ariel's eyes. As he rang the doorbell and glanced over, Ariel fled, her world tattooed ultraviolet, to the bathroom, which was glistening and humid with the smell of bath salts.

Ariel looked into the mirror, but could not see her eyes behind the sun's imprint. She ran a hand over the two clover-green strands in her hair; she twitched her nose, which bore a two-week-old septum ring that was for once not bothering her. As her vision resolved and the horseshoes faded, she saw her inflamed, swamp-green eyes in the mirror. She traced her hand over her belly, pushing against her t-shirt, and then removed her pop-bottle glasses and stood straighter. She contemplated the phrase "appearance is ideology," which some frog-Nazi had spammed on Twitter yesterday, and shifted her stance, unable to find visual peace. She started dry-heaving, seizing up in remnants of body-image problems that were supposed to have been brought under control by Dr. Larsson.

Knowing Bela would call her out any second, she blinked rapidly, waiting for her conjunctivitis to stop screaming, and then opened the bathroom door. A baritone voice came from the TV room, next to the bathroom. She lingered outside the doorway and entered. Bela and Rick, sitting apart on the chesterfield, turned to her.

"Hi," said Ariel, blinking.

"I'm Rick."

"Ariel," she said, moving towards him with her hand out. He shook it gently, weakly. He had a handlebar moustache like a 19th-century Prussian general, and she studied the slick mop of black hair buzzed at the sides. Ariel considered whether he'd snubbed her by staying seated, but she'd have opposed such a fraught formality anyway.

"So we had a tense episode with the neighbour," said Bela, who started into the incident with the Pomeranian. Ariel, who hated hearing retold something she'd just lived through, shifted weight on her feet, considering whether to interrupt the conversation or stir the *bigaos* in the kitchen, which was not vegan. Ariel watched Bela, who changed clothes about four times a day and had put on jean shorts and spaghetti straps. When Bela gave the story behind the Pomeranian moniker, Rick exploded into peaks and troughs of full-throated laughter—the kind that overconfident, wealthy men had.

Rick said, "Are you guys Polish?"

"Yes," said Ariel. "What are you?"

"Kraut–Anglo. My father was born in Germany."

"I'll trade you Szydło if you give us Merkel," Ariel said, smiling at her formulation.

"Deal."

Ariel smiled and then thought about this: "What?"

Bela stopped twirling her hair and left for the kitchen.

Ariel glared at Rick, leveraging her home-turf advantage. "Well?"

a. beaumais

Rick looked surprised. "Germany is always in the middle of outside forces. I guess kind of like Poland, but we actually, well, nevermind. It just seems like Germans are always marching too hard in some direction."

"Maybe you'd like our history instead, of being invaded and dismembered by foreign powers?"

"Um, sorry."

"It's not like *you* did it," she sneered. The truth was that Ariel, though born a Polish Catholic named Agata Ogórek, felt a dubious membership in the rank and file of oppressed peoples, due to her lily-white skin and the womb-obsessed, ethnonationalist politics of Warsaw. She would have gladly traded her ethnic identity for something more Brooklyn-chic; say, Ukrainian Jewish or Armenian.

"What do you have against Merkel?" said Ariel.

Rick laughed. "It doesn't matter. We just met, right."

"I want to know."

Ariel prioritized finding allyship over determining whether someone's apartment got morning sunlight. She and a classmate at Cell #281 had created an acronym, JILEBAFIRG (they were trying to come up with a better one), as a scorecard of issues—justice, immigration, labour, environment, banking, abortion, feminism, inequality, race, gay rights—to expedite this process. Ariel appraised Rick—his dog-whistles on race and immigration cast him in the reject pile. And that wasn't even counting the money he was giving Bela or the militancy of his haircut.

Bela came from the kitchen in an apron. "Is she harassing you?" she asked Rick.

Rick smiled as Bela bent on all fours to poke through a snake pit of electrical cords under the table.

"Gonna be seeing more of that tonight?" Ariel muttered a bit loud.

Rick shook his head. He was about to speak, but decided against it. Ariel relished the sight. Trolling a man paying her sister for sex: *yes, please!*

Bela plugged in the A/C, which filled the room with an airplane hum, the machine squealing and pinging like the seconds before an explosion. Bela dragged over the fan, which added to the noise pollution and rustled Rick's shirt at five-second intervals.

"I wonder if there's something wrong with the fan. Maybe the coils are starting to freeze?"

"Sounds like a job for you," said Ariel.

"Sure," said Rick.

"What tools do you need to do that?" Ariel asked. "Maybe we have them here."

"Arieeeeel!"

"What? He offered."

"He just got here."

"Well, I guess it can wait."

Rick stared at her—whether with incredulity or hate, she didn't mind which, although she was curious.

"So, where do you work?" he said.

"I'm doing my PhD at the University of Toronto. I write sometimes for *Buzzfeed*." She rushed to add: "My friend's a contributing editor at *Jacobin*. I just sent her something yesterday."

Rick's lips curled. He covered his mouth with his hand and looked off, faking a cough.

"What's so funny?"

"Nothing."

a. beaumais

"Where do you work?"

"*Free Speech*. Do you know it?"

That was it.

She sunk. There could be no meeting of the minds, no matter if Rick built schools in Haiti or sheltered stray cats. *Free Speech* was a nominally libertarian blog—an amalgam of Ron Paul supporters, incels, pick-up artists, neo-reactionaries, and all manner of misfits signalling against modernity. A megaphone for anonymous bile, it'd mimicked the glossiness of sites like Vox and Salon. Its lunatic cadre of racists had even mutinied to form an offshoot, *Hate Facts*, which had been disavowed, unconvincingly, in *Free Speech* editorials.

"So I guess that makes us enemies," said Ariel.

"I'm not a writer there. I'm just sort of behind the scenes."

"Is that supposed to be better?" She sat up straighter on the couch as Bela sat beside her. "What's your last name?"

"Speer. *Ess pee ee ee ar.*"

As she typed it into her phone, he asked, "Are you looking me up?"

"Uh huh." Actually she was sending his name via Telegram to N3MO, a pink-mohawked Oakland hacker with a starfish tattoo on his cheek. A teddy bear in West Coast DSA circles, he completed contracts for the SPLC involving social engineering hacks and data collection on hate groups. As for *Free Speech*—which had gained prominence with a notorious article on Obama's *alleged* plan to racially diversify U.S. neighbourhoods through Section 8 vouchers while prohibiting background checks on felons—N3MO could find out what connection Rick had to it, as well as any other dirt.

"I don't have a lot of Followers," he said.

Ariel copied his name into Google—5,100 on Twitter. "Not bad," she said.

As she scanned his tweets, which were mostly devoid of politics but had a jokey, channish flavor, the door to the basement opened. Jane's pink Reeboks stepped through and hung suspended, testing the waters, followed by her smiley, squinty, upturned face, weightless as a balloon. She ran to Bela on the couch, jumped in her lap, and stuck her tongue out at Rick.

Ron came down the other stairwell, downcast, eyes fierce and skipping around, his cardigan faded, motheaten, one cuff stained black. Ariel hadn't seen him in three weeks. His nose looked shiny and Macintosh-coloured, like he'd submerged it in ice. His walk was laboured—all sweaty regret. When he saw Ariel, he did a double-take and looked away.

"*Co jest na obiad? Bigaos?*" he asked, which Ariel slowly translated to herself as, "Are we having bigaos?" She'd stopped speaking Polish when she went away to undergrad at Sarah Lawrence, and had even resisted before that. Even *Jane* was probably better than her now.

Ron said something to Rick that Ariel couldn't understand. Rick stood up with his hand out. Ron stared at him from multiple angles as he shook it, as though computing the results of a psychographic examination. Then Ron smiled slightly with, Ariel thought, satisfaction and approval—more approval than he'd shown Shahzad at their first meeting.

As Ron crouched with popping kneecaps to forage in the liquor cabinet, Ariel looked at Rick and said, "Were you the one that published that essay years ago about the Obama Administration's plan to diversify the suburbs?"

"You mean 'Against Diversity'?"

a. beaumais

"That's an incredibly fascist title."

He smiled. "Are you always this nice to people you just met?"

Before she could answer, Ron was in front of them holding out vodka shots. Ariel didn't really want one, but when Rick plucked one from Ron's unsteady hands, she didn't want to come off as a simpering maiden.

"Where's Bela?" asked Rick.

"Doesn't like vodka," said Ron.

"Don't you know anything about her?" said Ariel.

They clinked glasses and Ariel took her shot, coating her stomach with a warm fire. BDSM movie frames and Google Scholar titles about desiring-production spun on parallel reels in the sieve of her grey matter. The A/C blasted her knee with cheap icy wind. Why was she putting up with this? Rick was a john paying her sister—was also a fascist piece of shit, the likes of whom she'd have shouted out of any classroom by now, if the prof hadn't. And yet she was drinking with him in her dad's house.

Just then, Jane—who'd been sitting on the floor swiping through pictures of firetrucks on her iPad—leapt up, stole the vodka bottle, and ran upstairs. Ron barrelled after her, his gut flying like a garbage bag of books, his *kurva* punctured by dog-like panting on the steps. Through the floorboards Jane screamed in radiant agony. Ariel stared at Rick. As he typed on his phone his neck and arms looked tyrannosauruslike, hunched in repetitive edgelord strain. The wailing crescendoed upstairs, Ariel's disdain for Rick competing with, and ultimately eviscerating, her embarrassment.

But the screaming continued and she asked, "So why did you print that, anyway? Just for clicks?"

Rick looked up from his screen. "Well, I don't know where to start. There's a lot to say there."

Ariel flexed like she could fight a lion.

Rick sat up, his eyes shifting to the right as he chose his words. "Lack of 'diversity' is treated as a panacea for all the world's problems. I mean, ten years ago, all the guys in balaclavas would protest globalization. Now they protest people protesting globalization."

Ariel reached for the vodka on the table, but did not take it. She did not want to give the impression she was drinking as a way to wash down this *totally dazzling* insight, which was a siren song of the privileged. So what if white men had to go to the back of the line sometimes? They'd ruined half the traditional societies on earth, and yet now *they* were an endangered species?

Ding dong.

Ariel charged mid-thought to the front door, sliding on the linoleum. She undid the deadbolt for Shahzad, for her reinforcement, who stood there with headphones over his fro—headphones he wore while driving, while shopping, while sleeping—and holding a bottle of Niagara Falls wine. He looked mellow, as usual, and she wanted to grab him and say, "Do you realize there's a Nazi in the house?"

He'd already kissed her on the cheek and shed his sandals and started to the family room before she'd even briefed him apropos of diversity and Section 8 housing vouchers. She went and watched the back of his head as he shook hands with Rick. She stepped nearer and glared at them, watching closely for signs of micro-aggressions, but Rick's face merely bore a smirk of social openness as he and Shahzad commented on the ninth-inning home run in the Toronto Blue Jays game (about which, notwithstanding baseball's appeal across socio-economic strata, she did not give the hottest fuck).

The steps groaned and Ron re-materialized with the sloshing, uncapped vodka bottle. Shahzad handed him the Niagara Falls wine and he took it with an ungracious nod into the kitchen. Ariel sat down on the chesterfield, sweating, potato pancakes reheating in the kitchen, from where a flurry of Polish emanated as she took the measure of the male bonding in front of her. She'd always considered Shahzad too naïve; even if she pulled him aside and apprised him of Rick's horrendous ideology, he'd probably just say it was *in her head*.

"When's your talk tonight?" Shahzad asked, perceiving her bad mood as she reached for—but pulled back from—another shot.

"7:45."

"Are you and Bela coming?" Shahzad asked Rick.

"To what? We're seeing Father Jack Rainy at the Port Lands."

"Father Jack what?"

Rick showed Shahzad a video on his phone and Ariel drank the shot. *Fuck you*, she muttered, suffering this moment as inspiration for a new feature (or at least blogpost to shop around) on race, the patriarchy, and dating.

Bela appeared aproned in the door: "Dinnnnnnnner!"

Rick and Shahzad started for the dining room and when Shahzad passed the door, he craned his neck back and said to Ariel, still on the couch, "You comin'?"

She nodded.

He winked, went off.

Ariel entered the bathroom and put down the toilet

seat lid. She sat, pulling out her phone. In her chat with N3MO, she typed, "That guy, you can hurt him if you want to." She waited to hit Send.

| The Ecstasy of Bela |

"We shall not talk about what we just saw," said Bela, "till the morning."

"It's not too late to go to the police," said Rick.

"I know, but there's nothing we can do this second and I don't want to ruin tonight. We already paid for the tickets."

"We could go to the police. What if he goes near your sister? You're crazy."

Bela and Rick stood in the drink line at the Port Lands behind a guy who'd used a full bottle of grooming cream in his hair and a girl dressed like Pocahontas in a leather headband and feathers. An indie rock band was playing, a blonde brother–sister duo on guitar and keyboards. Bela and Rick'd broken into the Pomeranian's house an hour before, and what they'd seen in the basement made her want to drown herself in the port-o-potty, but she also didn't understand it, didn't know if they could get charged with B&E. And besides, she needed to be out right now, needed this, she thought, as she started moving her hips. Despite how fucked it was, she felt excited, like how you did when the night was young and you'd had one and a half drinks.

Bela watched Rick pay for two tall cans. He asked the Spanish lady in a visor, "Two hundred percent mark-up?"

She danced, "Eet eez what eet eez."

Bela led them to a fence and sat on the concrete ledge in front. They clinked drinks and ate Portobello poutine in the shade. Bela looked back and forth from her food to the stage, to Rick, thinking she was seeing a shadow in her peripheral vision, a recurring hallucination spiked by the acid she'd done last night. Nonetheless, these few seconds were a good moment for her. She remembered how often she'd had good times tightly coiled with freak accidents. The day of her violent death, she decided, would surely be the sunniest day of the year.

A man with full-sleeve swan tattoos and a waxed moustache that she wanted to touch sat cross-legged on the ledge with a girl with straight bangs.

Rick stared at them. He said, "So what is this? What do you call this, is this a subculture?"

"What?"

"Is it like, in the past you had people who followed weird trends, disdaining everything that was too normie. But then one day, maybe after September 11th, the KKK cool kids club decided it'd be ironic and rebellious to admire the mainstream, Beyoncé, Taylor Swift, whatever. Now these people are the conquistadors of all culture and you're considered an asshole if you don't like something."

"I don't know," said Bela. "I guess. I mean, I don't like Beyoncé. Or whatever."

"Even this event," he said, "like, is this some kind of culmination of our society?"

The void in her sleep last night, the springs on Jerry's couch, scraped her tailbone. "That's stupid."

"Sorry."

"What do you expect from this?" she said.

"I don't know. Something more meaningful."

"OK, how about we pick flowers under a waterfall and then poison ourselves?"

"I know, I know. But sometimes it's just... just."

"What?"

"Just like, how do I put this: the industrial revolution and its consequences have been a disaster for the human race."

He burst out laughing, choked on a cheese curd. She handed him his can and he pounded it back, laughing a few seconds, looking insane for another few. Bela didn't find it funny, but at least he looked better when he smiled. She stared at the Toronto skyline with the CN Tower lit purple and red for the Raptors. People in her peripheral vision seemed to be drawing closer, unless it was the shadow-glitch, and, when they kept their course, she turned her head: it was her friend: was it? It was Silvia. Ariel's friend. She returned Silvia's wave and elbowed Rick: "What do we tell them about us?"

"What about us?"

Silvia was trotting over like a high-jumper about to

clear a bar, arms outstretched, compelling Bela to jump up and follow script. They hugged, Bela feeling Silvia's silky tie-dyed scarf as Silvia squeezed her. Silvia finally relented and introduced her two friends—Jess, a small-breasted girl in a bandana and bikini top, and Hernando, who had a Spanish accent and hovered around, tired and blinking out an obligatory smile.

"Hi!" said Silvia, centering Rick. "Have we been acquainted?"

"It's…" Bela looked at Rick. "…my boyfriend. Rick."

Rick's eyes rose in a wave that quickly crashed.

"How'd you guys meet?"

"Well, online."

"Of course!" said Silvia. "It's weird *not* to meet that way!"

Silvia gushed with cosmic festival energy that made everything interesting, as if she was on Adderall narrating a TV documentary—*like, Stalin killed a lot of people, but, like, it's all in the past and it was just kind of part of the times!*

They went off into the smallish crowd, following Jess, who rallied everyone with a plastic sword she held to the sky. Bela kept looking sideways at Rick for a read on what he thought of their "relationship." She'd tell him later that the reason she'd introduced him that way was because Ariel's friends always pitied her like her only skill was spraying OxiClean or sucking dick in club bathrooms.

The band played their last song. Rick said, "We're in a relationship?"

"Was that bad? I don't know why I said that, to be honest."

"Well," he said, drinking half his can. "I might be

open to it."

"Might be?"

"Well, if we're together, then we have to maintain each other's attraction levels at all costs. We can have passionate intensity, we can let ourselves go sometimes, but we must acknowledge that unless we manage this by maintaining a certain distance and detachment, then bubbles will form, which will kill things. We have to treat attraction like we treat money or sleep or food."

"I don't like that," she yelled into his ear.

"And I don't like working every day."

"So you mean you want me to push you away when I want to be close."

"Yeah, sometimes. If you come on strong and I don't reciprocate, you need to pull back. I mean, lab rats behave this way."

Bela finished her can of Sapporo and danced into him lightly, looking at the rip in his khakis, seeing how he responded to her rhythm. Or didn't. He seemed more into breaking and entering than dancing.

Bela: "But if we're constantly trying to outdo each other to be blasé–"

"Then we could fall out of orbit."

She nodded almost violently: "And it feels fake."

"That's because we're not used to treating relationships as having laws, except in a kind of lame pick-up artist way. People want the lack of regulation, they want to cry."

"Cry all day, dance all night."

He didn't respond to this. "They don't want to demarcate their feelings too closely because that's what robots do."

"I don't follow," she yelled over applause.

"It's like if this concert was kind of shitty, you could complain and leave and just burn all the money. But that wouldn't be pragmatic. So instead you manage your expectations, drink more, take more selfies, and later you'll tell people you had fun, or at least that it was OK. Or if the concert was totally amazing, you could lose yourself in it but then maybe you'd get bummed out in the coming weeks when your life was boring in comparison."

"That's not how it works," she said.

"OK, bad example. But just think of marriage. People get married and they take this leap of faith, they sign this contract that's against so much reason, and then they're unhappy. Why? Because they stop following these dynamics I'm talking about."

"I'm not proposing."

*

At the intermission, walking through walls of bodies lined up for the port-o-potties, Bela pulled Rick by the hand and cut through a pair of war-pig chicks with Coach purses, at which point Rick wriggled out of Bela's hand and turned his head from then, mouthing something in response to something they'd said, or just cursing life.

"What was that about?" she asked.

"I don't know."

"Why'd you let go of my hand?"

"Tell you later," he said.

She punished him by taking his hand again and swinging it apelike and ever-higher, which, being tense as fuck, he must have disliked, but he let her. They walked back towards the plastic sword, Bela thinking she had no right to hold his past against him—and she didn't actually care whether he'd fucked some *Kanadyjke* with an ugly purse. She wasn't jealous, exactly, but there was something beyond curiosity. She didn't mind the feeling of his hand, the veiny brittleness, the sense that he was an alien species coming into orbit with her. Maybe she could walk along the river with him at 4 a.m. He was good-looking but didn't know what the hell he was doing.

As Rick left to buy beer, Silvia asked over the crowd, "How long have you been together?"

"About a month."

Bela's need to explain was relieved when Father Jack Rainy walked onstage in black with black-clad band members. He looked like a bipolar Amish funeral home worker off his meds.

Stab me in the face, you can call me Sid.

Father Jack Rainy gyrated his hips in a Figure 8 as he strummed a guitar. He was the only celebrity she found hot. Bela wondered what he'd say if she met him, if he'd try to tear through her with bad jokes.

The permed keyboard player hit the first notes to "Shorn in the USA" and the crowd held up lighters and smartphones. Did his wife peg him like the one song said?

Bela looked at Rick and then backed herself into him, wrapping his forearms around her abs. He secured her and they swayed to and fro, Bela trying to get him to move more rhythmically, Rick's body (just a little bigger and stronger) feeling scientifically designed to fit hers.

She stared again at the CN tower, thinking about

a. beaumais

Rick's past, her past. They'd only met twice before at a coffee shop. She'd only ever had one boyfriend, a 40-year-old sax player she gave her V-card to her second year of university before he left her for a salsa instructor. She'd been reeled in at the after-hours club by tunnels of tenor, rings of sound splashing everyone in the dark room, where you bought drinks with little tokens like Pachinko balls. The way he had that non-verbal power that made people cry with his music. She dropped out of school after he betrayed her. She'd seen him on Queen West the first day of spring, had turned to run the other way, and he'd trailed her a block, pleading, "Let me speak!" She hadn't wanted to see his bowling-ball head, unlike before, when she'd implemented a black-out between them as a means to lure him back—a strategy that royally fucked her over, making her a magnet for his associations. It was worse than what Rick was prescribing.

There's no need to love me, darling, I hate you as you are... when you're alone.

Bela looked back at Rick, who was lightly rocking in an almost hypnagogic state, which pleased her to see. She felt vacantly vibrant, the clouds and sun playing tricks like when she'd use the fisheye mode on her webcam to make her tits look bigger. She felt like she'd lost the dial tone of herself and yet she felt OK. Rick looked at her and she thought about kissing him, but she turned back after a beat of hesitation. She waited before plunging herself deeper in his arms. She looked around—a butch girl in a Yankees cap smoked a vape and gave her the evil eye, as if they were crowding her— wondering what kind of bed Rick had, whether she'd lie in it tonight, having lain in so many to no end.

When you're frowning and beneath me, I can hardly believe

you've found me and I'm thrilled by that.

After the song, Father Jack Rainy pointed to the Budweiser truck bar: "Budweiser? That's so fucking stupid."

Silvia tapped through bodies along to the bass drum to "Bollywood Cemetery." She got to Bela, jabbing the sword in the air for a 20-second dance circle. Silvia said something and Bela couldn't understand even after two repeats, so she just smiled and drank the last drops of her can. She thought of grabbing Silvia's arm and saying, "Do you want to do sewing this week?" because she knew Silvia did sewing, but something stopped her, some knowledge that Silvia would agree but it would never transpire, some anxiety like a two-foot wall that made her turn back.

Silvia unzipped Hernando's backpack and pulled out a water bottle. Bela thought she saw a swirl of dissolved granules, unless it was a strobe effect. Silvia smiled and gave her the bottle in both hands, flat, as though presenting baby pajamas at a christening. Bela looked both ways and took a drink, remembering that she was on a date, at which point Silvia did a hand motion for "keep going." Someone grabbed it out of Bela's hands after her second drink. It was Rick, sucking down the bottle.

"This tastes like plastic," he said, his Adam's apple slowly putting through the order.

Silvia started laughing and then covered her mouth and neck with her palms, which made her look like Bane from *The Dark Knight Rises*. Bela pulled Silvia by the scarf, yelling into her ear: "What was that?"

"MDMA. With a twist."

Bela said, "Should I tell him?"

"Tell me what?"

a. beaumais

Silvia wielded the sword in the air and went off.

Someone's gotta help me, pig. Someone's gotta help me, pig. Someone's gotta help me, pig.

Bela watched Father Jack Rainy jump on the bass drum and shake his bony ass. She didn't know what to tell Rick. She had no idea if he did drugs. She countenanced the possibility that he would freak out, but there was no use lying to him if he'd had half the bottle, and it was his own fault anyway.

"It had a tiny bit of MDMA."

"Oh my God. Are you serious?"

His eyes pulsed and he looked around, sticking two fingers in his mouth.

"Wait! Have you never done it?"

"Fuck no."

"Why don't you see how you feel?"

"I don't want to end up with some dude's tongue down my throat."

"What are you talking about? I thought you were supposed to be badass. I thought you wrote weird things on the Internet. You've never gone to a festival?"

Her chirping seemed to get to him, the arguments advancing like lava.

"Do it for me," she said. "You broke into a stranger's house tonight. Are you telling me you can't handle a few hours of feeling good?"

He looked both ways, weighing options, and started coughing, as though to trigger puking, but then swallowed again and stood straighter, blinking hard, as though committing to the course.

FJR started his last song, holding the mic in one hand

and swinging the cord like a jump rope.

Bela tried to change the subject: "Do you think Father Jack is past his prime? His new album kind of sucks and he's always getting in political arguments on Facebook."

Rick didn't say anything.

"At least he's not a one-hit wonder," she said. "Or one of those artists who–"

"Who has a good first album and then makes another four with expensive production but no purpose left except trying to maintain a fan base that hasn't taken the hint he's never going to put out anything good again."

Getting high on this ratshit as the global market crashes...

Bela smiled, trying to think of some way to tie a ribbon around this topic, as a token of appreciation for Rick taking drugs. In his ear: "The key to Father Jack, to being any sort of artist, is the mask. The persona of a tortured asshole. The second he takes the mask off and becomes Tosh Stillman the person, he might as well be giving a TED Talk."

Bela wanted to listen to the end of the music, but Rick shouted in her ear, "I wonder if he minds that people don't want the real him. But with everything videotaped, there's nothing real left to preserve, and he knows that. So at least he's smart."

Father Jack Rainy played the last chord and the lights dimmed. The crowd did an exodus like a bunch of brats. Bela whistled and screamed and said a little prayer to the Creator if only Father Jack would play one more, pledging three days at the end of her life as an offering—and wasn't this walk-off-plus-encore just expected now?—but the kids had ruined it by leaving and she knew there wouldn't be one. Nevertheless, she looked over at Silvia and Rick and it dawned on her that she'd been left with the first rays of a burgeoning MDMA high.

She felt like an abandoned child in an amusement park. Bela could still hear Father Jack Rainy in her inner ear as the crowd thinned into stray colonies on the concrete. She followed her friends away and, if before it was like kayaking through a maze of rapids, now it was like circumnavigating ancient mossy pillars in the deep sea.

She remembered how she and Rick had planned to go to the police station in the morning.

The new chemical reality was altering that.

"Are you guys coming to Loft404?" Silvia asked.

Bela looked at Rick. He said nothing but his eyes said yes. They started to the exit by the lineup at the Korean-Mexican fusion vendor, Bela blossoming with peace even as she remembered what sick shit her neighbour had done. The ideology of serotonin.

She was thankful to have some MDMA suddenly imposed, that she couldn't get nervous over—molly seemed too easy a hack to not feel guilt over—so long as this was good stuff Silvia had gotten. She judged people over their drugs the same way you'd judge someone over their punctuality or hygiene. She could deal with a micropenis or a bit of poverty, but bad drugs made you as cool as Chelsea Clinton or Meghan McCain.

A girl in a beanie was paying a vendor when Rick said "oh shit!" and blocked his face with his hand. He looked sideways to gauge whether Bela had heard. She made sure her grin said that, oh yes, she had. They caught up to Silvia with her sword by a taxi parade. Rick said, "I'll explain."

"It's on Adelaide, between John and Duncan," said Silvia. She pointed to an SUV with gold rims and an Arab guy in a purple suit staring out the window.

"You guys can take this if you don't mind paying a business-class fare."

Rick opened the door for Bela and she grabbed his shoulder and ducked onto a leather seat. Rick climbed in and closed the door. "You have some explaining to do," she said with a huge radiant smile, like she was 12 years old in a caravan in starry Arabia, or Palestine, a caravan following the North Star to the manger. Rick smiled: "Explain what?" The driver looked back and said gruffly, "Where we go, folks."

Bela laughed, having forgotten the driver. "Hey," she said to Rick, but he was buried in his phone.

"What's the address?" Bela asked.

"Oh shit!"

For Bela, watching him on MDMA was like watching a wolf play with a baby chick. He told the driver the address and they pulled onto the expressway. The traffic was molasses, but she wouldn't have objected to an eternity like this.

"So, you want me to red-pill you on my woman situation."

"I don't know what that means, but OK."

"First thing is I *do* have a girlfriend. None of those girls at the show. Yes, I'm a piece of shit. Or, I guess I have two, now that we've consummated our love publicly."

Bela tore her mouth open with her smirk and took a stick of gum from her pocket, the flutter of sparks in her taste buds making her lick her lips. "Look, I only said that because Silvia doesn't take me seriously. I'm not some… jezebel." She smiled, she imagined, in a witchlike way. "I don't just clean toilets and do nails. I just feel like none of Ariel's friends take me seriously. They treat me like a lost puppy."

"Are you?"

She wasn't sure what he meant, so she just smiled out the window and then said, "Do you have a picture of her? Of your girlfriend."

Rick swiped through his iPhone, through wedding photos, resort photos, bridesmaid photos of a dirty-blond girl with a long large jutting triangle of a nose that made her look like an opinionated lawyer who had a mortgage and a pantry full of organic food.

"She's an app developer," he groaned.

He swiped through the phone till he got to some red-panties pix, a belly button glinting gold, more than a little enticing (Rick was *not* dating down). He shielded the phone until he got back to bridesmaid photos, breasts clamped by the purple cups of her dress. He cautiously rotated the screen towards Bela. The girl in the photos had no bags under her eyes, no runaway feelings. She looked upright and demanding and Bela imagined her calculating the price per kilo of broccoli or directing a construction crew to rewire her kitchen. She would not take Bela seriously if they met in person.

Bela thought this and sawed her jaw, but then treated herself to the observation that this girl was endowed with a slightly hulking forehead and mouth—to buttress her beefy brain—and sharp unground incisors that were vampirish when she smiled, which was not often in the pictures.

Bela said, "Can I read the last few texts she sent you?"

He surrendered his phone with a shrug, but his hand was ready to spring.

Telia: I was thinking about that conversation we had last week. there was one thing that bothered me that you said and I thought it would be good if we could talk about it?

Rick: What thing
Telia: What you said about priorities, with regard to what my
mom said
Telia: Where are you
Telia: Are we going to breakfast tomorrow
Rick: I don't think your mom meant anything by that
Telia: Can we still talk about it though

Bela cycled back to messages from unnamed numbers. She looked at Rick; he nodded, permitting her to click. One was a picture of two girls in pink gym shorts in a bar, leaning on each other with elbows jutted chickenlike. Another said, "im alone here bb 😳."

"Dude, you're throwing up red flags like a matador."

He flushed with embarrassment but didn't stop her from cycling through more messages.

"Wait. Are you saying *you're* judging *me*?"

"What the fuck does that mean?"

Silence. A bus honking at a renegade cyclist. Seeing herself from the sky, panning into inflammation.

"I've only ever slept with one man."

The driver, a statue among their ranting, turned around to look Bela up and down. She was not afraid of anyone right now. She felt like she was underwater in a cocoon with jet streams massaging her temples, even as she felt she would be impounded by walls of betrayal. She wanted to say she'd only fucked James three times and the first time hadn't worked, but she chose to let the men's judgment fan out and breathe.

"You know you were talking about sticking your tongue down some guy's throat, maybe you and this g–"... she didn't finish. The driver didn't flinch and she wondered if he comprehended as Silvia's magic water leapfrogged through her synapses and jammed any potential for confrontation. It wasn't the driver's fault anyway. She looked at Rick.

"I'm sorry," he said.

"I'll delay your punishment till tomorrow." She laughed at the writhing Medusa mass of cocks that Rick ascribed to her, a twinkling mass like stars.

"I can assure you that you're the whore in this vehicle," she said.

"No. This isn't who I am."

The driver pulled off on the shoulder on Adelaide and looked back. Rick said, "No, continue."

"All this degeneracy on my phone, I didn't mean to become someone like that. It's not who I am."

"Degeneracy?"

"Anything that inhibits human progress."

"Isn't busting a nut in a chick progress?"

"Not your average Tinder crazy."

"Where do I fall on that spectrum?" she asked, her stomach flying on a broomstick through a cloud of narco-turbulence.

He reached out his claw and they clasped hands, his fingers sharp and surprisingly small. Bela's vision was swelling into a glitch-art forcefield. She turned to look at her reflection in the window: her pupils were soaring and alien and did not fit the rest of her face. Molly had saved her life, but it always made her look like a UFO crash site.

"I never meant to go on all those websites," he said.

"And you think I did?"

"Well, I did go on them. I went on as a sociological experiment. The sugar-daddy sites. Maybe I wanted to get addicted." He looked introspective for the first time since she met him. "I used them past the point of research, but here I am. But if it's what it took to meet you, it was worth it."

They stuck their claws toward each other and clasped again slowly.

"Am I a research experiment?" she said.

He bent to kiss her neck and the driver shot them a look in the rear-view.

She sat up: "Why do you feel bad about going on those sites?"

"I help run one of the biggest websites for men and politics. All we do is rail against excesses in the current year. Most of our readers think of women as fallen creatures. But then we publish articles on how to game them, a whole encyclopedia on how to sleep with every nationality of slut under the sun. And I'm getting pix of some girl's vagina I've never met… It's like I'm a recovering drug addict who does a tour of high schools sharing his story to inspire kids but then does lines in the principal's bathroom."

"We arrive, folk," said the driver. They got out on Adelaide West at a dusty office building with "Herald" lettered in the window, maybe the old headquarters of a newspaper. Across the street, a firetruck pulled into the station as a homeless man passed. In the lobby below Loft404 they flashed IDs to a short guy with a turtle-shaped head.

"It's on the fourth floor."

The elevator arrived after a few minutes, two steps out of alignment with the floor, its lights buzzing and flickering. Bela and Rick held hands and entered. The elevator started to creep up. She didn't know what to say: they'd barely talked before tonight. *What are we?* The cable wobbled and went taut, the industrial whir skipping a beat. Bela smelled sandalwood incense that diffused like a blown dandelion as they rose up.

She'd always pictured herself with someone musical and local, not rich and unknowable. She wondered if Rick just viewed her as a womb for his progeny, as social proof for neckbeards. If he gave her a monthly allowance, if she could lie under his weird shade, if there were more states with him to ascend to—maybe they could make this work.

The elevator opened upon chugging basslines and an earpieced security guard who last month had thrown out a rapey Sigma male following her from room to room. Bela kissed him on the cheek and Rick took out his money clip to hand bills to a frizzy redhead in a corset that suffocated her freckled tits. Bela stared into their jiggliness and Rick waited for her. She felt like a little girl about to dive into a ballroom at Chuck E. Cheese or McDonalds—Scrooge McDuck paddling through his gold safe. She took Rick's hand and went slowly towards the Skittles strobe hues. This was a test for him, she decided, and she would give him a report card.

The first room was playing slow minimalist techno and Bela didn't recognize the DJ or the people. She pierced her hand with a laser, catching it in her palm as a guy with a blue beard and a blinking WWE Championship wrestling belt crossed. She looked at Rick, who was already at the door to the hall to the next room. Minus one point.

The hallway connected to old hardwood rooms with mirrors and antique bookcases, one with a clawfoot tub with three people spooning. Bela and Rick blew like a jet of exhaust upon the main dance floor, where Matt Von Wilde in his Mad Hatter Hat spun jungle house. She took a step forward and felt herself crystallize, felt many pairs of eyes alight on her in a way she welcomed, as though offering herself at a shrine. She wouldn't have minded seeing Silvia even. She recognized people, but she closed her eyes and a voice, as though tapping the back of her head, told her there was a lot going on in her life, that she was treading in a hot-water pocket in the Arctic and that if she strayed too far or lingered too long, she would freeze. She remembered Rick Speer like a crossfire among the ambiance and opened her eyes to see him entering the final room with the bar. She told a girl she liked her fury gilet and then tapped Rick on the shoulder at the bar, docking him points for abandoning her but giving him a temporary exemption. She turned to the smoothie stand, read the whiteboard: *Awakening, Phoenix, Revival, Angelic*, till settling on a *Nightcrawler* with acai, quinoa, and passionfruit. She hesitated to order. On MDMA, she was afraid to break the ice, although when she did she couldn't shut up. (When she talked to people high, she often felt the next day that she'd harassed them, because she often *had*, asking them to speak Japanese when they looked Japanese but turned out to be Chinese, or offering drugs to some lonely yuppy who only resented her for breaking their mono-person in-group.) The smoothie-stand owner was her friend's cousin, but she did not bring this up, just held out the money and placed her order with a clean smile, hoping her pupils weren't sucking in the whole world and that she was able to determine the change—2 dollars—he should give her. She wanted to plant herself by the DJ like an old tree and just sway to the sounds, but Rick was nudging her back to the hall and she was too high to swat him down.

They went into a little room and Bela fell back in a nest of downy pillows on a purple velvet sofa. She wanted to take her clothes off and get in a hot tub.

"Where did we leave off?"

Rick shifted his jaw and brushed off pant crumbs that, to Bela, seemed non-existent.

"What do you think of this place?" said Bela.

"This place. One time I accidentally wandered into a place like this in Russia. But it was less gay. It was for oligarchs."

Bela did not want to think about Russia, for it brought her father's rants to mind.

"What's your girlfriend's name?" she asked.

"Telia."

"Am I going to become her?" asked Bela.

He hesitated: "I think so. I need to get away from her. She's good to me, but we're not on the same page."

"Why?"

He looked at her intensely and suddenly looked away, as though she'd caught him staring at her.

"I'm a culture warrior but she's apathetic to all that. Which I like... but for the wrong reasons. I want her to be apathetic because of apathy. But she's apathetic because she's too busy going to Women in STEM conferences and doing Python on Coursera. The second she takes the time to read up on anything and opens her mouth, I just want to die."

"Why are you with her?" asked Bela. She felt adrenaline cresting in her heart, like she needed to dance or detonate.

"You want to hear my theory? My theory is you shouldn't date someone who's more than a 7 out of 10 unless you're a sultan or an idiot. Because of jealousy. And second..." He shook his head, his pupils rolling like marbles in the red of the lamp. "Nah, I can't tell you."

She slapped his arm: "Say it!"

"Only if you tell me a secret too."

"But then we have to go dance. Seriously man. I could talk to your grandfather's grave right now. But I want to dance!" She slapped him close to the crotch, which made him jolt up. "Mine is probably worse than yours anyway."

"Fine," he said, drawing breath. "When I started going on those sites, like, SeekingArrangement, it gave me a kind of rush to tiptoe around Telia getting these pictures from girls, planning my next tryst. Like if I was single it would be desperate and sad and I wouldn't have the patience for it, I'd just be depressed I was single. But because I have a girlfriend it's forbidden fruit, it's something I juggle with my excess mental capacity, and girls smell it. It raises all my boats even when it destroys me."

"I should tell her!"

"Don't."

"My phone is dead anyway."

He took out his iPhone: "All these billions of high-time-preference bonobos ordering food and fuckbuddies to the door 24/7. The idea of just not doing something, of having a negative opinion about consumption, it's anathema."

This was not the direction Bela wanted to go in. Sitting here like this on MDMA was like putting on a ballroom dress to buy smokes at 7-Eleven.

"Okay, I'll tell you mine," said Bela.

"Let's race to the bottom."

"Well, yours is like that. Mine not so much." Bela did not know how he responded to insults. "I told you I haven't seen my mom in years. She went to Argentina to live with a plastic surgeon. The last Christmas card, from two years ago, had a Florida return address and some money."

a. beaumais

"So now you're the mother figure?"

"I got so angry at her I started to wonder whether she was my real mother. People say I don't look like them." Rick nodded in agreement. "So I took a 23andMe and got Jane to take one. She loved spitting in the cup."

"Oh, I know how it works."

Bela lost her train of thought as banana lasers lapped against the hallway wall. She felt like she'd slid through a trapdoor into a new phase of the drug lifecycle where she was splayed out on an operating table with the molly irradiating the amino acids in her eyes. Why was she sitting here talking about genetic tests? She remembered: "So our mitochondrial DNA groups were the same, which means our mothers are quite likely the same—"

"I know how it works. I've gotten six different tests."

"High five," she said, clasping his hand. "That must be the first thing we have in common, right? Buying genetic tests."

"I think so."

"I also got Ariel and Ron tested. I said it was 'genealogy research.' But the real reason was that Jane's test was so different from mine that I thought we must have a different *father*. And then Ariel's test was like Jane's, and my dad's was pretty similar."

"What did yours show?" He blushed like his face had a boner.

"It showed Polish but a lot of, um, you know, Siberia…"

"Yakut? Lapp? Mongolian?"

"The Yakut was absent from theirs but it was 22% in mine. Even the traits were different, the earwax, the sprinter. I had one copy of this mutation in the BCS-something gene but they didn't. I ordered us tests from another company and it was the same shit almost. And it's not like I don't look a little Asian if you look at me from above."

"No wonder you work at a nail salon."

"Fuck you." Bela stood up: "Dance with yourself tonight."

"Please."

"You don't even know how to dance," she said, "and you want nothing more than a reason not to."

Rick's face went wrinkly and flappy like a Basset Hound's, and Bela wanted to grab it, but she hated him right now, on a microscopic but ocean-deep wavelength.

"I didn't mean it as an insult. I stan Asians. Asians are good at visual tasks. Computers, ping pong, Photoshop. By the way, what's your Neanderthal admixture?"

"My dad is 2.9% and my sisters are 2.8, but I'm 3.6."

"I salute you, Neanderthal master-race."

Bela thought of the war she'd seen on TV between tall, warlike homosapiens and stocky, beetle-browed cavemen. How would a Neanderthal act on Methylenedioxymethamphetamine if they couldn't talk?

"So you're an orphan," said Rick, "with your mother gone. Not knowing who your father is. Did you try to find him?"

Bela shook her head. "Ron's my father now. I don't even know if *he* knows he isn't. Whoever my real dad is, he didn't stick around. Plus he was into my mother, which doesn't recommend him highly."

"Did you tell Ariel?"

"No. She was pissed she didn't have African DNA and only a tiny bit Jewish. If I told her what I found in my test she'd turn it into an essay. I'm pretty sure she doesn't know any of it."

Rick laughed deep in his belly and Bela imagined him

laughing at a skinny kid in a locker room.

"Your sister…"

"What about her?" Bela was not averse to Agata-trashing—Agata, who'd abandoned Bela to raise Jane, as she wrote articles from her apartment about autism. (Jane was featured humming and throwing mud for a few seconds in a *Vice* special.) Still, Bela did not want to hear his laugh again—maybe even felt a shiver of protectiveness over her sister—and so did not tell him that Ariel's birth name was Agata Ogórek, or that she sometimes wrote under "Ariel Ogberg."

"Your sister is an exemplar of white women in the current year."

"Um."

"Your sister thinks everyone can just work at a media company and take part in some passive Internet revolution to put down the drawbridge and extend the franchise to all of humanity. The whole impossibility and laziness of the project is what elevates it to a religious level. She'd ridicule somebody who believes in creationism or won't vaccinate their kid. But then she'd assail you with equally stupid beliefs."

Bela closed her eyes; kaleidoscopes hatched.

"It's just all dildo-pluralism. She wants to be a mother hen, in an armchair, pumpkin latte way."

"You're a horrible person," she said, turned off by the phrase "dildo-pluralism."

He shrugged. "We're all just riding our own wave, we're all social engineers. You, though…" He looked at her in a doctorly way, nudging her chin up delicately. "Everything makes sense now that I know you're an orphan. Your lack of a father. Would you describe yourself as a girl surrounded by mostly guy friends?"

"Not really. More like a girl surrounded by guys who want to bang me but aren't my friends."

A fortyish guy in a kilt and his girl made for the couch, startled when they saw Bela and Rick.

"Why hello! Good tidings!" said the guy. "Do you mind if we use this mirror?" The girl was reaching under his kilt.

"Not at all," said Bela. "We were just talking about genetic tests and dildo pluralism. Now we're going to dance."

The girl's cheeks dimpled with her colossal smile, the kind of all-purpose smile Bela gave when she didn't know what someone was talking about. The girl said: "You mean PLUR like peace, love, unity, and respect? Like, LGBTQ+ rights in EDM?"

"Exactly," said Rick, leading Bela away before she could say anything else.

"Is there a Facebook group for that?"

"It's in the bathroom," Rick said.

At the bar, Rick bought two beers.

"Hold your horses," Bela said.

She drank half of her forgotten, mostly full smoothie, which had melted in her hand. She offered the rest to a bug-eyed, quivery guy on the dance floor who kept removing and donning his shirt and looked like he was going to detonate. She took one of the pilsners, unsure Rick could handle himself, and led him by the hand deeper into the dance floor, which was teeming like a squatter house, purple nets of light bisected by yellow bananas. A couple made room for Bela and Rick, the guy saying in a butler's voice "right this way," and when they planted their feet on their own square footage facing the DJ and Bela moved her feet, casting off leg irons, it was like a force (she pictured a sperm) swam down through her leg (originating in her pineal gland) and she wondered why they hadn't done this the second they got here, but she was glad to be here now in their own private archipelago that could end any second if the drugs or the sound technician pulled the plug.

Bela nudged Rick lightly on the shoulder and he chugged a bit and she put her hands on his shoulders till he moved with her. He had dark eyes and a chiseled grandfather hawk face. The sounds transmigrated through her stomach, gravity delayed, Bela putting her head back and sighing so long, unable to believe that she'd met someone—had she?—no matter what he looked like in the morning sun. She put her hands on his hips and she spun them like a wheel of fortune to unlock their rhythms. He was like an 18-year-old who'd left his mother's house on a first date.

Near the "No photography" sign, Bela watched a permed strawberry blonde in a headband dancing. The woman had taken two of the many balloons in the Loft and tied them around her wrists, her long, black-clad legs and balloon arms gyrating in cunnilingus alphabet patterns. Bela went up to her just to be closer and the woman came to her, creating a bicycle motion with her hands that cast an electric force over Bela. They looked at each other till the woman said something about "happy" and when Bela said "what?" the woman pulled a balloon down and said, "This is Happy" in a northeastern European accent.

Bela turned around. Rick stood there almost slobbering in a way that'd be creepy if she didn't know he was high as fuck. The blue beard with the WWE Championship belt said something to him. Bela waved him over and the

European girl said "how cute!" Rick looked puppylike and confused, and, sensing that he had nothing to add, the European woman turned around and returned to her prior state of carving bassline triangles in the air with Happy.

Bela felt her brain flicker with a doppler effect, a sudden isometric hallucination of standing in a dance floor, removed from her body, time dragging her by the hair into the future. She felt like she'd lost a physical dimension and she held out her hand to Rick, who took it. He pulled her close and he stank so good, his lemony deodorant a halo around his misanthropy. She smelled him and he, for once, slunk a bit, let his posture down and mingled with her.

She looked around as he looked around. A guy in a cab-driver cap was looking at them. She wasn't ashamed as she put her arms around Rick and looked him in the eye, in the part of him taking her in under the shadow. She undid his cuffs and slid his sleeves up, stroking his forearms. More people were staring and she put his hand on her back and moved closer to his face until it was a fuzzy presence so near and welcome that it was like it wasn't separate and she puckered her lips. There was a movement like a stirring in his lips and she moved her head forward and paused it on his, letting their surprising coolness suffuse a second and transfer her a bit of moisture until she decided to take it from him, whatever was owed her. She thought of dancing in the Baltic as a little girl and draping herself in a skin of seafoam. She thought of Telia and whether they'd get along. Her brain created a sort of pink-splashed, linear graph of Telia's personality that she could interpret but not explain to herself. She could only compare it to the green, chaotic graph that she rendered for herself. And then she tried to make one

a. beaumais

for Rick but there was something occluded, or maybe it was light yellow and misty, and she put her tongue out and he opened his mouth and released a beer vapor like the smell of her one handsome uncle who slept in the spare room before her mother left, and she felt like she knew Rick, but she knew no one knew anyone. She slid her tongue in his mouth and he closed his teeth slightly to tame it and then he slid his in hers and she did the same with her teeth until they fell back on shallow kisses and met again more lightly. She tucked her chin back and looked at him. The DJ was mixing in the intro to Bowie's "As the World Turns," the masque from *Labyrinth*. She wanted Rick's taste buds again on her tongue and she took it as he said, "We're going to have a good future," and she wondered if this was being streamed from her REM sleep. She put her arms at the nape of Rick's neck, slow-dancing, but she moved her feet faster. Rick smiled and she could feel this being strung to the ball of five or so memories that formed her identity, could feel the aura casting light over the coming days, like the aura of a pleasurable migraine. Rick said something and walked backwards before turning to the bar. There was a short-haired woman DJing and Bela went up to her and said she was the greatest of all time and the DJ thanked her, putting her palms together and closing her eyes like a nun in prayer. Bela wanted to freeze this moment forever, like pausing a horror movie on the one hidden frame of a lily.

She leaned against the wall, people-watching during the downbeat, the culmination of her 15-year-old obsession with MDMA. She still couldn't believe a scene like this existed. When she was 12 she'd log onto Dutch drug forums and scroll through pictures of empathy-enhanced people who'd achieved a beautiful crumpled wonder as they watched the sun rise after dancing all night in a warehouse. She'd avoided trying molly for a decade, having read that it would splice her nerve endings and leave her perma-tired and hungry like black spots on her soul. But when she finally did it, she realized that taking it once every four months was more therapeutic than daily Effexor. It was like uploading her memories to a removable hard drive, formatting her brain, and reinstalling everything. Half of her thought process would be purified in the coming days, but there was always the suspicion that something had changed, that the contents had shifted during the flight, the slightest hum not there before.

She clenched and lined up to buy water as the DJ handed off the decks to an Asian-looking guy in a straight-brimmed cap.

Rick came to her. "I can see why you do this," he said in her ear. "At concerts, everyone stands like zombies waiting for their feeding. But this is like some primitive Mesolithic ceremony. And this drug. Just… just."

*

Ninety minutes later, her knees feeling blown out by dynamite, Bela took a three-quarters-full tall can from Rick, put it on a ledge, and led him by the hand through the hallway to the couches. She was getting a chill. Two of the three couches were taken and the purple velvet one had space for one body. She let Rick sit and she sat on the arm.

A BBW with an LED tiara who reeked of Flowerbomb was being repeatedly told by her smaller friend to "believe in yourself" as the friend swayed her hands in some California Dreaming luau way, even though it was trance through the walls. The sight of Rick sweating made Bela sicker, like she'd snorted a rhinitis spore. His forehead looked like it was slathered in sunscreen under the Caribbean sun. Bela reached for a tissue in her pocket and dabbed his head, but this only made him mad.

"What did you do to me?" he said.

"What are you talking about? You *grabbed* that bottle out of my hand."

"Yeah, I didn't expect you to put fucking psychoactive chemicals in your water."

He burped and inhaled with a swoosh, as though his stomach had a little vacuum inside.

Bela felt disconnected from her fingers, flipping her palms over and down again. She wondered what the fuck the "twist" was in the water. She should've cut Rick off after three drinks, because he clearly could not hold his own— although she knew there was something to be said for having experience with drugs, for having teetered hundreds of times on the edge of psychosis and vomiting.

"I'm sorry you don't feel good."

A guy with a shaved head, backpack, suspenders, and boxer-briefs came into the room. Bela couldn't tell whether he was more some rarefied gay fashion autist or else a perverted street guy who'd jump on any eye contact like a fly on shit. She rubbed Rick's forearm to distract him.

"I can't go to the police in the morning," said Rick.

"That's okay. You might feel better."

"What are we going to tell them? That we met on SeekingArrangement?"

Rick looked at the boxer-briefs guy. Bela wanted to

tell him not to stare, but she felt a great wall rising between the two of them, the U.S.–Mexico border.

Rick muttered something that tapered off.

"What?" Bela asked.

"Nothing."

"Say it."

"So am I supposed to pay you an arrangement?"

"Fuck off," she said. "Why would you say that?"

"What, isn't that the deal?"

She waited a moment, as though pressing her face into a blank white wall. Then she shook and a tear fell down.

"Can you calm down," she said.

"I feel violated. This is *not* OK."

She thought how even in a world where you might get kidnapped or run over by a car, she could not count on anyone for refuge even for one evening.

"I needed you to be different," she said.

Rick writhed on the sofa like a worm on a sidewalk.

"I'm sorry you feel that way. I don't like me either. But would you rather it took five months to figure out who I am?"

The couches swelled with refugees from the dance floor.

"Part of being human is to hide the shitty parts of yourself."

Rick said nothing, splayed back in discomfort, his gaunt, pimply belly winking under his shirt. Bela pitied how ugly he looked: how low his form could go.

"You act like you're living in some unrestrained way but your life is a lie."

"Honestly," he burped, "I don't know why you're mad at me. Did we not meet on a disreputable website? Yes or yes?"

a. beaumais

Bela loathed his snakelike voice, as though she were some Facebook comment being deconstructed. The way he marshalled all his venom to make the world her fault. Even if he said something that made sense, she'd fight back, she decided, because he was dismissing her, and she'd bleed herself dry before she let another person do that.

The guy in the boxer-briefs perched on the other arm of the sofa and looked at Bela. She wondered why everyone had converged in this room. She hated them all and everything was severed and snipped and convulsing, like the foot bath massager at the salon when it malfunctioned and the mechanical limbs hummed for nothing, the empty vessel's clicking noise.

"It's not what you said, it's how you said it. The way you brought up this 'arrangement' when you didn't have to. The way you blame me for feeling like shit."

"So it *is what* I said."

Bela shifted a few inches on the ledge, away from Rick, until she was sharing breathing space with the wall and some girl with full sleeves who looked pissed off. Bela looked across the void to Rick, his large, flat forehead greased like a frying pan. She noticed that she had no desire to argue with him, that she was not even sad yet, that the sadness would take a few days.

"Come back here," he said.

Bela stared at the wall, on which tracers crumpled and uncrumpled like candy wrappers. She hadn't seen Silvia in the Loft except for two minutes, but she hated her for the "twist," a twist of the knife in her brain.

"Bela," said Rick. "You don't have much going on in your life…"

Her chest lurched and she considered elbowing him in the face.

"…but neither do I. Well, I have a condo and more ability to milk resources out of the environment. But I like being around you, we could lean on each other. We could live in the Alps or something. But you'd have to accept me because I'm not sorry and I'm never sorry."

He looked so piggish and diseased that Bela didn't think he could pay a crackwhore for an arm wrestle. But she did not want to do him a favour by telling him this, did not want to get between silence and eternity. She felt a ghost limb of fascination that he could be so awful.

Clapping came from the main dance floor. Bela imagined pursuing Rick to a thatched cottage in the mountains, where she could escape her family and send them care packages every few months. She could study Japanese and live near a sauna. Maybe she could finish her last year of school as a child grew inside her, as she crawled on hands and knees through the dirt as she always had, low-down and close to the earth as she would for the rest of time.

She looked at Rick and didn't know where she was.

"This isn't normal," she said.

Rick tsked. "Nothing's normal. You have a smartphone, right?"

"It's dead."

"Well, if you have a smartphone then you're not normal. You missed that opportunity. We're all…"

"Not normal."

"Huh."

"I get tired of your commentary. It's all some rationalization for your sexual frustration. You have no idea how to talk to women. You don't even know how to dance. All it takes is a bit of enthusiasm. But you're looking around like the world is some museum."

His line of sight focused a second before returning to wiggles.

"Bela, congrats on this analysis. I'm sure you'd be a really clutch partner if I ever want to, you know, water plants or play Ouija."

"Fuck you. I'm leaving."

She shivered, the dam of pent-up self-hate crumbling under her tears, her face raw and cold under Revlon.

"Wait," he said. "Don't go. You're right about me, everything you say. And I wouldn't let anyone talk to me like that. But get real for a second, the deck is stacked against you. I'll message Telia and tell her it's over. I'll help you with the mortgage payments. I'll find Jane a support worker and we'll go to the police. I'm fucking sorry."

Bela thought of Oscar, a black tabbie hit by a station wagon before entering ultraviolet convulsions. She started to sob and the tattooed girl asked if she was okay. She could feel, on a time delay, her hatred of Rick converting into a more low-level, familiar hatred of the world. It wasn't that he'd seemed like somebody she could huddle with in a warm refuge against the outside until he'd shown himself to be shit. It was more that he was the Arctic wind itself, a modulated computer voice telling her she wasn't enough. He could serve no more purpose in her life than pushing her to withdraw into the invisibility she craved—more likely, pushing her to charge at the nearest electrical socket with a fork.

"I need you to do one last thing for me," she said. "I need you to call me a cab and delete my number."

"No." He burped and covered his mouth, leaping from the sofa and barfing on his hand beside an antique horse. He looked back in her direction, not making her out between his flooding eyes and puke hanging like string cheese. "Wait," he yelled, "wait," stalking into the hall. Bela got up, but couldn't see him behind the wall of people in the hall, people with high self-esteem, who, if they'd ever experienced anything like this, had gotten it out of their systems years ago. She returned to the couch, where some guy sat like a hen incubating rotten eggs in Rick's seat. He jumped up, almost knocking her over, and she reclaimed the seat—toasty. Bela watched a girl with a large block head and hyper-focused eyes behind problem glasses. If you were a doctor or lawyer, she thought, you just leapfrogged the lower halls and qualified for better partners. And if you weren't respectable, but you were reasonably attractive, you could still find decent specimens and gradually trade up. But Bela was not respectable—she did not register on anyone important's radar and merely straddled a low rung of girls who posted vintage clothes on Instagram. She could not hope for anything but future sad trajectories with wiry, sick-minded Internet men with shitty jobs and dysfunctional relationships with their dicks.

A guy with sunglasses and a beater and a five o'clock shadow was inching closer to her on the couch—unless she was paranoid—his arms stretched in a cycling motion in the air, in some drugged yogic posture. Bela's eyes were weighted by marbles crashing down. Strung out for the third time in two weeks. Deep under her skin, under the synthetic melt of eyeshadow, there was a little girl's voice crying out for childhood, or just for self-destruction, crying out for the fact that she wanted to be delivered from this but had nowhere to go, crying at the drumming of trance in 4:4, a marching band in cyborg hell.

I need to get out in the world, but what did this mean? Not getting high and sleeping till 4 p.m. Maybe she could take on extra shifts, buy a plane ticket to Japan, and have enough left to pay for a PSW for Jane while she was gone. Bela already knew the *kana* scripts and 800 *kanji*. She had an app.

A bearded guy in a cape squeezed in beside the beater guy and when they offered Bela a line she hopped up from the couch, berating them with her inner voice, but there was nowhere to hop to and she had to tap her way through bodies. She averted her eyes in a state of bawling and not existing, and heard a voice, maybe her own, ask if she was okay. After a minute, she asked the people in front of her if anyone was lined up for the bathroom, and it turned out that no one was, according to the facial expression of one of the staff collecting empties, so she barricaded herself in there, locking the door, re-locking it.

In the mirror, Bela took a strand of hair and then a clump of her locks, trying to refashion it to fit her jawline, but she looked haggard, her eyes schized out and puffy, her jaw bulky after so much sawing, or maybe she was gaining weight. She saw a preview of her future self as someone knocked on the door. She started removing her eye makeup and shouted "wait a second!" as a male voice said there were plenty of mirrors in the other rooms.

She took a breath and he started pounding, and when Bela opened the door she stared at the guy and he looked back insolently till putting his head down and going in. *Kill yourself.* The dildo pluralism girl's eyes hit on Bela in the hallway, and Bela put her finger to her lips as if she was sneaking around the living room on Christmas Eve. She'd never seen the Loft this packed before, and when she returned to the room with couches she didn't see Rick, but saw a fresh wave of fucking Toronto douchebags hollering and reclining, trying to jumpstart the night.

Bela went into the hallway and paced around. She cut through bodies to the bar. Past two guys kissing, she thought she saw Rick ordering something. He downed a water bottle and passed the bartender another bill, the bartender raising her hand to level with him, maybe about the dangers of water intoxication, and then he took a phone call, did a 360-scan, and started walking back to the entrance. Bela followed, three-dozen bodies between them, the DJ playing an ambient track to clear the dance floor. At the exit she nodded to one of the bouncers, the one who'd saved her from the supercreep, and saw the elevator closing, Rick's Swatch glinting, disappearing. Bela went down the fire escape, wondering why he was leaving, why she was following, what she should say, whether she should say anything at all, or maybe this was the best ending possible. When she got to the street, she saw him sticking his head through a cab window and opening the passenger door. He looked more sober than 10 minutes ago.

Bela breathed in the wet, exhaust-pricked air, stepping out of the way of a procession of suited-up, loudmouthed Toronto men marching to a victory beat. Bela thought about what it'd be like to snatch up one of these assholes—could she even?—as she hailed a cab. Rick hadn't thought enough of her to say goodbye. She waited five minutes until someone picked her up—her worth. As the cab turned onto University Ave, she saw her life framed behind glass and it was like a rat-chewed watercolour, a winter funeral with no one attending.

a. beaumais

She would not dangle over the rabbit hole of disturbed men on the Internet who could only alter her life in disturbing ways. She would stop going to clubs, which gave her nothing but the occasional envelope when she worked the coat check or brought bottles to a table. She would take on more shifts and work harder on her *hiragana* and conjugation until she could get a loan and go back to school. She would take Vyvanse when she had a heroic shift. She would go to the police station in the morning, alone, first messaging Rick, but probably not. She took out her phone to compose a goodbye message that she knew she wouldn't send—got the no-battery flash. She resolved to be someone who kept her phone charged at all times.

Bela heard nothing but crickets as the cab sped closer to Rosedale. The driver lingered at the bending three-way stop where cars often skidded and crashed. Maybe, after checking on Ron and Jane, she would take a walk in the ravine and sit among the trees, waiting for the sunrise and reading manga on her phone.

When the driver said "hmmm" she untangled the red and blue lights from the memory of the Loft's strobes. A police car was in her driveway.

| The Redpilling of Rick Speer |

The door blew open and hovered, almost closing before flying open again, buffeted by winds, a tropical electrical storm. Rick Speer stood in his housecoat in the hall, not knowing if the lightning flashes were in the world or in his head. Who had opened the door, and why?

His mind flickered with senility, trying to find a signal among the static, and when he found a channel, it was, "*I am in my apartment, and the world is gay.*" He shut the door and checked his phone—an act that didn't ground him or restore his vital signs so much as plug him back into the bright blue glow of Sponsored Content and status updates high-beaming the fetal ball of his cognition, a symbiosis close to what it meant to be alive in the current year.

"Where are you?" Telia had texted at 7:49 a.m.

"This is the last time," she'd written at 11:02 p.m. "I hope you're having an amazing night wherever you are! Clearly, what you are doing is so much more important than me!"

The little twister forming on the sea of Rick's moral sense did not have a witness in the plaque of his consciousness, and so it died. He'd learned to leverage these low points in his relationship with Telia in order to accent the peaks, rather than chasing the dodo of a "happy, sunny relationship" or whatever the hell they talked about in the Russian novels he fell asleep reading. Mostly, he did what he wanted, seeing girls from the Internet behind Telia's back and then, once the winds got too rough, showering her with sweet texts and attention and facing down her threats till one night she was lying under him, parting her rusty locks once again and telling him she loved him, at which point they'd reached the next phase of their sunny relations, framed by a knowledge of trauma and a history of collaborative overcoming.

His mind was dripping like the AC he'd fiddled with at Bela's. He felt like his mental searchlight was unable to devour anything. There was a reason you didn't take MDMA if you were somebody. Besides promoting extremely gay thoughts last night—lending answers to life's impasses that were no more realpolitik than Bambi gallivanting through the meadows—it'd tattooed his grey matter, lasering his short-term memory like hairs in a Groupon session.

Rick Speer lay in bed, feeling dozens of feet below the floor, below the planks, in the cold earth. He picked up his phone again. He needed a VPN like Bela needed an IUD.

It was only the morning, or the early afternoon, but already he felt like his phone was a ghost limb, like he would need to scull through the day on little boosts of notification dopamine.

He had bruises on his neck and didn't know if Bela wanted to talk to him or if he wanted to talk to her. Last night, when the Pomeranian pulled the Glock out and stuck it in his mouth, Rick had promised he wouldn't talk to the police about what he and Bela'd seen. It was all gauzy and maximally fucked up, fat deposits transubstantiating in water, all these coiled insides of Bela and her family, Bela and the party, Bela and the Pomeranian, Bela and Telia. He did not know where he stood with her, and a larger part—or at least his id—didn't care. But he felt in the *not caring* the footprint of serotonin leeches.

His Lake Shore apartment was a convection oven tickled by Freon; he was empty. He could not achieve death by jumping out the window; maybe a broken ankle. He said to himself, *I'm bleeding...*, a mantra he'd whisper when he looked out at the void, which he was old enough to know not to plumb, for it led either to the emergency room or a hooker's perfumed embrace. (He couldn't think of a situation— funerals, his aunt's cystic fibrosis diagnosis—that wasn't overshadowed by a hologram of his dick, by the impulse-opening of an Incognito tab with Sugar Babies and Craigslist, or an 18-year-old Moldovan on a webcam.)

This is my struggle, he'd say to his four real-life friends, not knowing what was worse—the shockwaves through his life of having no self-control (especially as a half-German!), or the hypocrisy of editing a men's webzine that ran three articles a day excoriating "degeneracy" and sexual licentiousness.

He went to the kitchen to pour himself a glass of

water, then another.

The water could not breed stability. His ruminations were a spiral staircase to a resinous dungeon with candlelight flickering over sleep-sapping repetitions. He scanned his faculties: he was a bit hungry. He felt no direct sexual urge; his testes were inert. His blepharitis was overshadowed by brain damage. His heartbeat was surprisingly light, and he did not feel as groggy as expected. He got distracted taking his pulse after five beats. The real question was the woman question, the question that kept on hatching new versions of itself. He edited a file on his phone:

```
Telia - Bad fashion - 115 IQ - 42-28-38 - Dutch,
Scottish (Beaker) - Mid Beauty - High Economic
Usefulness/Agency - Maybe Child rearing - BAD
conversation - High Neediness, Blah sex - Obama,
Kanye West, accounting, Python, C++

Bela - Good fashion - 107 IQ - 37-26-36 - Slavic
/ Siberian, Yakut (high Neanderthal, high EHG)
- High Beauty - Low economic Usefulness - Child
rearing yes - Neediness? - Sex? - Party, drugs,
music, dancing, Japanese
```

Rick wanted to start a family in order to create a productive prison for himself; he wanted to send sons out into the world to fight the rising tide of high-time-preference degeneracy. (If all the last men became remedial teachers in a critical studies class headmastered by the Zuckerberg dynasty, why not commit *seppuku* now?) He'd given Telia a "pre-engagement" opal ring, though he wasn't sure he wanted to commingle with her genetic matter and risk the passing on of her love of

Beyoncé, notwithstanding her Mensa brain (he rated her IQ lower than what Mensa had, which rated it 133), as well as the manifold advantages of her being a Woman in Tech.

He'd never had sex with Bela, he thought, collapsing on his bed, and therefore didn't know her, but having a SeekingArrangement profile painted a black mark on her forehead (he was aware of his double standard; he knew he deserved to be thrown out of a helicopter).

As he lay back and stretched, he started feeling more mentally hygienic, as if someone had unscrewed his brain casing, vacuumed the dust, and streamlined the wiring. But when he nodded off and his brain entered pools of false-alarm dreams (more just ephemeral flittings of the dance floor) till he really was sleeping—doing breaststroke in a stone pool overlooking an orchid-lined fjord and shooting his arms out and scissoring his legs froglike—he sensed a karmic shadow darting across the pool floor, or was it his own? As he summersaulted into the wall and kicked out, an infant hand gripped his ankle. He stopped kicking. He could not see anything in the pool but sunflecks on the surface. He tried twisting his head back, but the hand adjusted its grip and he spun in circles. He used the other foot and kicked at the hand, hitting a small torso. He kicked at it again and torpedoed forward in a frenzy, squeezing the kid until the hand pulled him underwater, and he fought to resurface, drawing air, but the hand dragged him to the bottom of the pool and he cracked his hand on the concrete, chugging water, opening his eyes underwater and seeing the child, a beautiful burgher boy in Alpine Swiss suspenders killing him.

He woke to the sound of crashing glass as his skull went through the bottom of the pool. The crinkling continued

a. beaumais

as he drew consciousness and touched his head, thankful it wasn't busted open, thankful he'd achieved a few minutes of brain-defragging REM. He lay panting at the stucco ceiling, more optimistic he was going to recover from MDMA and from all his bruises, even if he was still a few feet in the earth. He went to the bathroom to piss a radioactive stream, and when he went to the fridge to pour a new glass of water he noticed the broken window. A rock shaped like a distended brain sat on a kitchen tile. Rick didn't know whether he wanted it to be real or a serotonin syndrome glitch. He picked up the rock and it felt evil. He put it on the counter, broomed up the glass beneath the curtain. He turned on the light and the rock glared as though hexed by a Javanese shaman. Who had done this? The question metastasized but his sympathetic nervous system stayed offline, as if the order to register an emergency would take a few hours. He was more preoccupied with the shape of the rock than with a potential vandal or home invader. He unlocked the balcony door and stepped out under the cicada-rattling sun, the misty blue spidering his floaters. Only a Cirque de Soleil acrobat could break into his third-floor apartment from outside. The rock-thrower, if there was one, was probably some bully on a stolen bike. He went in and put on his sunglasses and bathrobe. He took the elevator down to the lobby and nodded to the receptionist, who half-nodded back, and went outside. There was no one in the parking lot or on the bench beside the pond. Rick paced the parking lot and looked at his window on the third floor, as if performing forensic calculations about angles of rock flight, but really his mind was a dumb concrete ocean, beneath the surface of which there might have been swimming some paranoia about whether Bela had done this, or the Pomeranian, but not really.

In the lobby, waiting for the receptionist (of Indian origin) to get off the phone, he wished he could fast-forward to a time when he was rested and detoxed, with an intact window, an espresso, and an essay to upload on *Free Speech* that would fall like a guillotine on Twitter and Facebook.

But instead he was waiting for Ramesh, the nametag said, to stop talking about Bashir's burger restaurant MBA project, with what Rick suspected were metaphorical references to *Game of Thrones*. Rick remembered when Ramesh first stepped off the plane last year. He'd worn an orange turban and paper-bag suits and let sharp scruff grow on his cheeks. But now he was a fly dude, with custom suits, exposed hair, eyeshadow, and, in all likelihood, wicked Tinder game. *Toronto is the urheimat for westward Asians*, he'd read on a BBS. While New York, notwithstanding its wage-serf class, priced out everyone but sheiks, Tribe, and the China Construction Bank, and while London was a European capital with a colonial legacy that blunted the high notes of multikulti Hosannas, Toronto was in the goldilocks zone: ugly, post-historical, and Anglo-Presbyterian, the hub of an underpopulated frontier where within a few short centuries the polite, forgotten, principled imperialists would become polite, principled diversity-strengthers, slightly less forgotten. Their mayor would ordain Menstrual Hygiene Day.

"Sir? Sir."

Rick jerked himself from his slack-jawed meditation. He took off his sunglasses, but this made everything look washed out like a bad viewing angle on a TN monitor.

"Hey. Someone threw a rock through my window."

"Room number?"

"301."

a. beaumais

Ramesh typed this into his computer and flipped through a notebook, the LED lapping at his sclera. He clicked a few times, and Rick wondered whether he was looking up *Game of Thrones* summaries. It was like he'd asked to settle a bar tab.

"We can send someone this a.m. Will you be on location?"

"Yes."

Ramesh nodded.

"This will be covered by my condo fees?"

"I'm not sure, sir. I shall look into this circumstance."

"Thank you so much."

Ramesh grimaced and Rick went to the elevator, wondering if he looked like a raver. Perhaps Ramesh could x-ray his reptilian thoughts. Probably Ramesh was too upmarket for him. Upstairs, he unlocked the flat and lay in bed, calculating how many generations ago he and Ramesh, a North Indian, shared Caucasus hunter-gatherer ancestors. He didn't know why he was thinking about this. Well, he *was*. It was the kind of slithering rumination that powered him through his daily struggle.

The epochs of his life were marked by spurts where he'd leapfrog to new obsessions. This had surfaced at age 10 with wall-touching (he had to touch one wall if he touched the other). This had migrated into an obsession with reading and properly comprehending every word on a page, until he got a "satisfied feeling" (often too tepid to stop him from re-reading the previous page). This had migrated into the more socially acceptable yet still maladapted pursuit of Magic the Gathering and D&D games. This had migrated into a running–powerlifting–creatine phase, which made possible his short-lived courtship of a Hyperborean Yamnaya Latvian girl with a factory-made phenotype, whose cheating on him despite his washboard abs and ever-ready wood (which she never touched, besides grinding on it once and another time giving him a three-second handjob as they watched *Aladdin* with her cousin) led him to bitter bookishness and a Freud phase. This had migrated into cutthroat, zero-sum academic warfare against his peers, the quest for 100s and IQ-boosting nootropics and, eventually, stimulants. This had brought him, fresh out of Adderall, to buy what was described on a BBS as "bathtub modafinil" before his final stats exam, following all-nighters in the library, which resulted in him shouting *ho-, ho-, hot* as if licked by flames while he itched and shook with erythema multiforme and got carried away on a stretcher, although he unlocked the belt and ran alongside the stretcher to the ambulance. The school administrators hadn't let him do a makeup exam despite an appeal and, one course short of his bachelor's and his dad refusing to buy him a lawyer unless he got a job, he'd impulsively moved to a town near Heidelberg in Germany to live with an aunt he'd met once at an airport cafe.

Meh. In bed he scrolled through his email from the time he moved there. There was a guy he'd met there named Oscar. Or maybe an Asian girl named Akoya. Someone he wanted to remember—someone who could do something for him—who could tie a bow on his ego, get him laid or teach him easy metaphysics. Maybe Felix's sister—a serious Catholic? (He felt like at least one of these people didn't exist, and he blamed Bela's drugs.) *In 1130, the Neuburg Monastery was established in the Neckar valley. 06/12: The bishopric of Worms gained influence in the valley, founding Schönau Abbey in 1142.* An email from a walking-tour company. He remembered how

a. beaumais

Americanly dressed he was when he stepped off the plane, his spring jacket two sizes too big, forehead oily. He started learning German. He thought of applying for dual citizenship and grew obsessed with the European Union, his birthright, the politics of integration and accession. Some of his best memories in life, the kind of sublime depravity he identified with, spawned from his walks through the medieval market square at 4 a.m. entranced by German-language mp3's and old Namibian-German foreign service dispatches he'd found on IRC, a stream of tendentious political speech gushing through his pleasure center, like he was the lion of Brussels bringing Eurosceptics to heel: *Ov course, vee should move past a currency wunion zoo a viscal vone, because a two-track Europe vill condemn ze projekt ov integration. As gut Europeans vee must veech an agreement wiv Greece and ze other PIGS countries, vone zat preserves ze dignity of ze Germann taxpayer.*

He would cross the border into Poland for a week and then return for three months and do it all again, but after a while the German border started drilling him and he decided to fly back to Canada. At brunch he wanted to rock out with his cock out about Hohenzollern Castle or the Frankish ethnogenesis, but Toronto people asked him about refugees, about the photo of Alan Kurdi washed up on a Turkish beach. He didn't get it. He'd always preferred Europe on a somatic level: the pastries, women, long naked legs, palaces. The way they practiced sustainability and sex over bling bling hedonism. But with the boats sinking, the Europeans were sitting ducks led by an octopus of technocrats waiting for things to get worse—people who were so fucking bored they *wanted* things to get worse. He was all in favour of a Romanian coder not using a condom with the girl he met in an Amsterdam hostel, or a Persian linguist becoming the chair of Vandalic declension at a local college. You had people crossing borders between the greatest cities on Earth—but the people in his imagination rode bikes and drank espresso and maybe even talked about Simone de Beauvoir or Goethe.

He'd noticed the first burqa in town in the weeks before leaving Germany—had noticed his Hochdeutsch reach parity with a kebab seller who'd been there a decade. There was just no way it would work. No, he'd say to his friends in Toronto, there was no way the European navies wouldn't send the boats back, build camps for women and children, get the Americans to stop bombing. But instead, the Germans let CNN bullycide them all summer. What for? There was nothing the Germans even bought from America except Hollywood movies, iPhones, and treasury bonds. Maybe the people on banned subreddits were right. Maybe the E.U. was just an American province managed by German industrialists, just a net for beautiful slaves to get caught in and buy cellphones and debt: a tributary state with opulent buildings and a dead-on-arrival information economy.

08/19: FREE E-BOOK: Your Facebook friends are wrong about universal healthcare. The summer of his return, living far from any robust welfare state, no matter the articles he read (when he should have been jobhunting) about the Christian Social Union and the Party of European Socialists, he started dabbling in Ron Paul and Mises forums, reading bitcoin newsletters and venturing out to hotel-basement meetups in sad Detroit exurbs hosted by fidgety, benignly seditious eggheads, nerds united by a bulging conviction that there had to be something beyond this bread and circus for the lowest common denominator, the slow suction black hole of fractional reserve banking, clownworld, and endless wars for McUniversalism. Rick posted a Blogspot about Helmut Kohl and the Basic Law, which he'd researched for five months and which got two likes on Facebook. 10/18: *MONSTERINSIGHTS: 10,000 VIEWS!* But then "Blockchain and Digital Libertarianisms," which he'd basically scribbled to himself as a round-up of current thinking and hyperlinks, got 240 retweets and almost 7,000 pageviews in four days. The editor of *Free Speech* started following him on Twitter and asked him to write a bimonthly column on "anything to do with cryptocurrencies, AI, and liberty," which he didn't know about like he did E.U. politics and Otto von Bismarck. But he was living with his mom, so why not? *03/28: JOB POSTING: ASSISTANT EDITOR, $32,000/Y.*

(He wondered if he'd find the girl he was looking for in his e-mail, the trad-Catholic, maybe her LinkedIn or Facebook. Maybe she didn't exist. But it was better than searching the Internet for prostitutes.)

He climbed up from columnist to contributing editor to assistant editor. His articles sucked—he didn't know theory, no matter how many times he used the word "semiotic." But it was all just gamified social media—right time, right place with the rise of candidate Trump. When he took over as assistant editor, the most productive hour of his tenure was when he configured SEO and paid $9.99 for a new site theme, replacing the cursive font and low-res parchment-yellow background—which aped a Declaration of Independence aesthetic—with a mobile-optimized Times New Roman theme.

He deleted the Eagle and the American flag except for in the "About" section (and even here, it was downgraded from

GIF to JPEG) and implemented a house style guide that limited to five the per-page frequency of the words *liberty*, *freedom*, *constitution*, and *Declaration* and mandated decapitalization of *liberty* and *freedom*. Pageviews rose as *Free Speech* looked less like a backwoods militia site coded in the nineties. Rick intuited that a movement—especially an online one in the age of cookie-cutter John Oliver psyops—had to soar like a fireball above the culture, too hot and fast for normies, too beautiful for the gold souls not to condescend to. It didn't matter if you had official endorsement of ideologues so long as you were getting retweets, so long as people felt connection.

Nonetheless, Rick's growth mindset met opposition from the old guard. *Free Speech*'s executive editor and owner— Marvin Myers III, a bowtie-wearing marketing consultant and purveyor of home-school curricula who, besides his interest in property rights and Austrian monetary policy, spent most of his time raising his six daughters—was too congenial to voice a disagreement that Rick sensed lay camouflaged in his spectrum-y mores. Marvin was conciliated when *Free Speech* dropped Google Adwords in favour of a libertarian-run platform for libertarian-vetted (they didn't use that phrase) ads.

Rick could let accusations of liberalism from Tea Partiers and patriots slide, even the occasional hater's memes about *Free Speech* selling out.

But what brought him to a spiritual crisis—almost a Ted Kaczynski man-in-cabin meltdown where he didn't leave his chair, answer emails, or do anything but eat lentils and play *Starcraft 2* for six days—was that in the thousand-mirrored snowflake debt-binge of Western civilization, where the Kardashians were the aristocrats, libertarianism, which he somehow now devoted his days to, seemed merely to be the queasy, gentle, inept cousin of ruddy fat Texas conservatism. It could only attract bronze souls—the terminus of live-action roleplaying for photophobic, seditious, aspy, dirty-minded man-children who so rejected *muh big government* and *muh welfare* that they mistook the desert of NIMBYism for magic dirt. *Everyone can manufacture dildos and enrich their own uranium as long as I don't have to pay for roads.* In the hollowed-out beehive of neoliberalism where academics, media, and elites advocated hatred of the middle and an ever-roiling rug to be pulled out from below, you had a society that was as far from libertarian as possible. Rubbing their hands over crystal balls, the brahmins of the American Empire controlled the globe through the export of woundedness, of low-level, malleable ethno-religious strife under whose veneer of free markets and civil liberties the strings of social progress were pulled, where capitalists could rebrand their export of jobs and trashing of the commons as a paragon of openness. The ballooning American Empire had to fill the world in its pews or play out the apocalypse. It had to line up seven billion to hear its bubblegum symphony of promised reckoning, or it had to pop. Libertarianism was just a little boy opting out by staring at the wall.

He knew the Trump train wasn't his hill to crash on. It all felt like a phase. He'd not thought much about politics through high school and university, besides, like most people, giving it more thought than it was worth—although manosphere hustle-porn and getting called out by a few women for language indiscretions (or paranoid shit they *imagined* he said) had seeded something venomous. In Germany he'd temporarily turned the page on whatever that was, as he was too busy learning German and studying the behaviour of large south German men with their complex, mythological noses and mildly crazed, strabismic eyes that animated their severe fairytale nature. Rick missed talking to a tweed-clad professor in Cologne who spoke of Schiller and Fichte and Reinhold and gave lectures at the library or a coffee roaster's, sometimes drawing prisms to represent Goethe's theory of colours or sketching Swedenborg's flying machine—lectures that cost nothing and where everyone shut up and listened in some totally foreign-to-Rick display of "pure learning." He wanted to be back on the Continent but his passport application had gotten rejected because his photocopied driver's license said Heinrich, not Rick. For a long time since, in the Toronto condo he'd bought with his uncle's help, when Rick posted contributor essays about rent controls or the housing market, the comment section was anything but tweed-clad, was mostly IQ charts and happy merchant memes.

Few wanted to talk about quantitative easing when they could weigh in on the IQ level of hill-tribe-descended refugees in Minnesota ("*Yeah, I know these people have been fucked over for millennia by surrounding empires, but when you have an 85 IQ that's what happens, I'm sorry*"). Such comments did not disappear with new blogposts on passivism or ending the Fed, or with the angry backlash by Tea Party types who, though disavowing the "race pill," ratcheted up their anti-government rhetoric and allusions to civil war.

All this was a wick burning down to the European refugee crisis, which exploded like a barrel of nails and put *Free Speech*, which had crawled since the Ron Paul defeat of 2012, back in the running. Here you had the West stuffing its foot in its mouth and eating it, backwashing biological warfare, with Western NGOs organizing incursions in Turkey and Libya, whose leaders blackmailed European leaders, who blackmailed the European middle class. As Merkel took selfies and shepherded her flock through the Brandenburg Gate, it was impossible to get eyeballs on "Strauss and 18th-Century State Rights" or "A Propertarian Reappraisal of Alexander Hamilton." As the migrants threw rocks at Hungarian police en route to Germany, Rick couldn't stop wondering how life was back in Speyer, in Karlsruhe? His aunt said the villagers, who'd welcomed their quota with cakes and spare beds, were now turning their backs after the schoolgirls started getting their butts pinched.

And when Rick pulled the trigger one day on an overpriced ticket to Heidelberg and pulled into the village bus station after a 26-hour journey dotted with cancelled flights, he found a bunch of men in tracksuits standing outside the turnstiles, licking Cheetos dust off their fingers and drinking wine from the bottle.

After he got to the public pool and made it through a queue where the staff used the translation function on their phones with a bunch of not-Syrian men who insisted on no German and no payment, Rick dove off the diving board and spotted a brown speck. On his return lap he noticed it again in the waves: a water world of shitty diapers. He almost started crying, but he didn't trust his impulses. He tried pacing downtown at night listening to mp3's, but it wasn't the same with all the men sitting on the steps and benches watching him. He returned to the airport two days later, this time for good. Germany was no longer an exotic map for his VR machine; it was just an expiation chamber.

dox

*

05/22: DDoS attacks on Free Speech: A mutinying intern, later traced by his IP, had copied the *Free Speech* CSS and set up a nearly identical site called *Hate Facts* that published screeds against the "shitskin rapefugees" under pseudonyms like "Pigmented Summer" and "Intersectional 1488." Though Rick signed a *Free Speech* editorial denouncing *Hate Facts* and trying to force its intern–founder to deny, by threat of doxxing his name, any connection to *Free Speech* (they deleted this threatening clause after a morning of Azerbaijani DDoS attacks), he maintained a once-removed connection to *Hate Facts*. He listened less to German vocab mp3's than to the Saturday Night Lies podcast. For about a month he referred to himself as "goy" in conversation, though he stopped when someone pointed out that whites calling themselves goys was the same as blacks calling themselves negroes.

As the days got longer, he'd take road trips to New York or Chicago listening to neoreactionary podcasts on Nietzsche, Strauss, Deleuze. He felt like he had a place in the world, that Trump was a light—however deficient in its spectrum—to grow towards. It made it easier that he didn't have to invoke the welfare state and devastation of the family unit to explain inner-city crime; these were just "chimp-outs." You didn't have to write essays against neoconservatism when you could call out wars for Israel. You didn't have to long for some Taco Bell-worshipping Wild West of saloons, Bibles, and free markets when really what you wanted was a white Japan. If you tried to hold out on the outer ring road of multikulti, they would come for you eventually. The state would break up and bus your neighbourhood, would seize your kids and pump them full of hormones and Facebook. The blue-checkmarked blue-haired freaks would do their jihad (and they liked jihadists way more than they liked you). They would cause civilizational collapse so long as their political pets threw rose petals at their feet and the billionaires kept the gangbang going.

*

09/05: MEETUPCODE: 928238. It wasn't that he wholesale "took the red pill." He'd attended, with fear of his picture being taken, a bar meetup in Toronto affiliated with Lauren Southern (mostly because he wanted to bang her, or engage in some ironic far-right BDSM). He left before she allegedly arrived, but in the meantime, he'd gotten a random sample of the Twitter right—which, while containing more of a multicultural Mike Cernovich-tier manosphere representation than that by white identitarians or 4chan performance artists pursuing a school-shooter aesthetic—nevertheless revealed some quirks, like how many attendees, despite being surprisingly openminded and sharp, were clearly in the throes of the "woman question," having devoted hard currency and psychic energy to pheromones, *Gorilla Mindset* ebooks, and whey, such that if a woman looked at them they'd either ejaculate or have a two-week panic attack conciliated only by constant Internet postings on "game"—something many of them tried to rebrand in their online postings with incel jokes in an effort to dissemble the fact that they were not crazy mad scientists, but crazy mad virgins. A few other attendees, he found, were Twitter trolls of the ironic-race-war-now stripe who'd engage in "Is *x* group white?" discussions and cryptic ethnogenetics, always with a negative verdict, always declaring outer-Hajnal whites wogs, in the name of joy if not accuracy. Many of these personas who were the loudest voices to weigh in on the purity of the Silesians or Highland Scots were of mystery-meat stock. There was even a turbaned Sikh who, though looking more like a typical Punjabi than a blue-eyed Buddha, high-energy joked with a deep podcast-y vocal tear and a vodka Red Bull in hand that the original Sikhs were Aryans and that anyone not descended from Harald Hardrada should be "put in an oven."

These men were not of Mayflower stock. For if you descended from wealthy Anglo-Dutch industrialists, you were too market-thirsty to shun Big Diversity. If you descended from Puritan cultural elites, then you were co-founders of the pozzed religion of Judeo-Saxon brahmins. If you were phenotypically North Sea–Kurgan with sandy mammoth-hunter hair and Black Sea blue eyes, you were way more likely to be lying in a tent at a music festival inseminating some Mestizo cutie than shitposting Pepe memes about the rising tide of autism—let alone siring a Lutheran dynasty of Kierkegaard-reading engineers imbued with the "Faustian spirit."

The other people at the Lauren Southern meetup were Christians, mostly trad-Catholics who blogged broadsides against "degeneracy" and tweeted Michelangelo art layered over vaporwave. Some wore ties and were impressive in a two-and-a-half-dimensional way, with connoisseur knowledge and a semblance of the kind of community-oriented thinking required—and yet in such short supply—for a new rightist civilization. And yet during their second pint together, when one 18-year-old monarchist with a fake ID who wouldn't shut up about Evola started slurring words and stumbling, and kept bringing the conversation back to "sodomy," maybe with regard to some girl who'd cheated on him, or in regard to gay people, or maybe he was self-hating and closeted, Rick had to excuse himself to the bathroom and avoid this monarchist, saddened that despite seeming somewhat impressive, the guy was seeking some kind of ordination and facing some sexual questions that it was not Rick's job to answer.

*

At some point between indulging these people and wishing he could delete them like his Internet history, Rick had to admit that, though he hated anarcho-capitalists, PUAs, 1488ers, trad-Christians, accelerationists, NEETs, and Nazbols—he hated them half a degree less than the general population. It was just too easy for normies to believe falsehoods and become human shields for consumerism. People and plants and dogs and the sexes were not the same. Man had developed separately in the jungle, in the tundra, by the sea, on the mountain, in the city, in caves. Man would develop separately in space pods, in test tubes, in lines of code. To say otherwise only made race and sex realism into samizdat, into a nipple ring you could secretly rotate when you were bored. You could see the cognitive dissonance in genetic-testing kits, which revealed your separateness down to whether you carried a Neanderthal allele for sneezing after dark chocolate but whose commercials showed everyone as octo-racial, with freckles, an epicanthic fold, a flat nose, a copper afro. (Rick was penta-racial, at 46% Germanic, 40% Celtic, 6% Balkan, 6% Ashkenazi, and 2% Broadly Southern European.)

He saw the logic of racial agnosticism, but people

were too greedy and stupid to settle for it. Focusing on race was not what any healthy civilization would do any more than a straight man would genuflect to his straightness. If you were Jewish or Chinese, there would always be a paternalistic faction of central planners that herded the sheep away from the cross-current of the capitalist shredder. But whiteness was fragmented and spent, with no sword left except the shopping mall. Whiteness had been beaten to a tin pulp, to something that could assert itself only through winks and shell games.

He'd long thought of himself as a genetic winner whose *noblesse oblige* and pragmatism, not to mention all the Colombian women he bent over on weekends, checked any race-war urge. But gradually, with his $32,000 per year as an assistant editor, his failed sojourns as a day-trader, his poisoned money-making ventures—his inability to break up with Telia—he turned the scope on himself. He noted his low impulse control, his slavish adherence to a mediocre post-industrial life, his broken family. He moved out of his mom's after hitting up his petroleum-engineer uncle for money, started seeking wealth creation rather than just renting out his time. But the more he cultivated self-awareness, the more he inched closer to the plain sight and smell of his defective genome, the burgeoning sense that something was wrong with him on a congenital timescale, that he was a wignat in racial quality if not politics. It was like the lone knight defending the castle against the Nazi skull-measuring doctors had committed suicide in the moat. He got more genetic tests. His ancestry ran from the low end to the high end of white servitude. His mother descended from Scottish and Cornish United Empire Loyalists: farmers, city councillors, lawyers, sheep thieves, some mentally deranged people, one prominent whale watcher. Scottishness was a black box from which you could pull out anything: you could playact a kilted bog-poet or Whig philosopher or Revolutionary sea captain who fought an armada while penning calculus theorem by candlelight in the Bay of Bengal. On the Y side, his father was a German immigrant from a line of Junckers, pastors, and people expunged from the record. He'd been called Hitler in the schoolyard, which had bothered him before he found an illustrated *Art and Iconography of the Third Reich* in the public library one morning and felt a testes-like stirring at the runes and panzers, Verfügungstruppe stormtroopers and Welthauptstadt, beside which the French and English colonial uniforms in the history textbooks, which they wore during all the battles over who gives a fuck on the Saint Lawrence, looked scarecrow-like and primitive. His family would take trips to the Black Forest and camp along the Necker and Rhine in towns far more aesthetic than the hegemonic strip-mall civilization he'd grown up under.

He took more genetic tests and got more depressed. He wondered why Germany was so strict and severe in a way he yearned for. Why his love for that guttural robot tongue that made the trains arrive on time?

In Germany, as he got into European politics, he'd felt, lacking the words for it, that the land of his father was one of strongheaded, trampled-on people who, carrying the 4000-year-old scars of a forced busing in the middle of Europe between western and eastern tribes, were distinctly devoid of humor or the ability to let their guard down, a rigidness that was no match against intense psyops by the British, the French, the U.S. State Department, centuries-old lassoing by jealous, gasping, resplendent Anglo-Normans.

It was only when he saw the shit in the pool that he stopped thinking of Germans as perfect fallen beings. And when concert halls got shot up in Paris and the Germans banned dissent on Facebook, then it was like the scab of his mortality had been picked at and was spurting up into the void.

If it was true that Nords had built high-trust conformist ecosystems, then it was true that if you hacked the firmware, you could make them extend the franchise to strangers in ▮▮▮▮▮▮▮▮▮▮. You could titillate them with the CNN spotlight and they'd pay in blood for a crumb of the cultural radiance that, being progress-oriented volk, they starved for.

One day he drove to Grenadier Pond and sat in the rain, his fishing rod extending like a dead tentacle as his hand rattled rhythmically. He needed to stop thinking about his dad's family. If they always charged too hard in one direction or the other, if they wanted to be the cow shit in which a consumer class grew, then it was not on him. And yet the feeling of his own racial inferiority, the knowledge that there was no way to win, made him not colourblind but only more obsessed.

*

Rick rolled over in his waterbed, wedged in a sewer of ruminations, new tides of dirty memories washing over in a way that was suffocating and drug-fueled as opposed to natural and sleep-inducing. He was well practiced in controlling his breath and trying to keep still to quell runaway thoughts, having long seen them as bubbles of fatigue, fear, or degenerate thoughts that should not be further inflated, even if this meant stymying sweet, creative manias. He did, however, allow himself to brainstorm blogposts in the shower—*auf Deutsch*.

But thought control was not guaranteed under the influence of drugs.

Rick decided he was awake, but he waited the requisite five minutes before looking at his phone (a self-improvement guru on YouTube had called this *refusing to surrender your sovereignty*). He grabbed it and saw a Twitter message from one of the managing editors of *Free Speech*: "Are you okay?"

"Yeah," he typed, putting on his slippers. "Why?" Did he know what had happened with the Pomeranian?

It was noon, Rick saw, knocking over a congealed ketchup bottle in the fridge in search of milk for cappuccino. He could not find any and could not will a quarter-litre into existence by re-searching the door and vegetable drawer. The problem: he had a lot of shit to do and could not drink his coffee black. He had to reach a full gallop of wagecucking—somehow. In the kitchen he leaned with one hand on the island and wrote in his phone:

```
-redbull, milk
-wait for windowmann
-email telia
-thot board inquiry?
-respond to emails
-css
-ephereum article
-jack off?
-gym
-bela?
```

He added *kale, blueberries* and considered whether to place the jacking off before or after the gym. Before—because then he could work up a sweat and shower off his alienation before seeing Bela. After—because then he could avoid feeling effete at the gym, hairy palm haloed. Before would be optimal but would require going out in public with a masturbation mindset. Not jacking off was the most chad, but he was a cognitive husk. He realized that he might have to use what a 4chan friend called *hyper-deep-cell stimulation* (a dopamine flood achievable via porn/sexting or violent videogames) to really wake up for a few hours, and not jerking off required dragging himself to a coffee shop and brute-forcing through his tasks before returning home to an early night of emailing his accountant or, at best, sexting SeekingArrangement girls in his sweatpants, although he needed to wait for the window repairman and, ultimately, he knew that the trad/pre-frontal-cortex thing was to see Bela today, if she'd talk to him, and maybe even see a doctor because he couldn't turn his neck without a popping.

Rick stripped down and traced his lower pecs with his index finger in the mirror, seeing how, attached to his cognitive junkyard, his chiselled body bloomed like a Miltonic garden, notwithstanding the wine-red bruise on his neck. He stroked his uncircumcised Alemannic member to nothing in particular, then to wholesome and loving feelings directed at Bela, which he quickly abandoned in order to sit on his gaming chair and recall the vivaciousness and red lipstick of a raver girl last night, but he could not get erect, despite a tingly blue fuse in his balls, a rousing that called for alleviation or alienation if not today then tomorrow.

Rick assumed the window repairman could let himself

in with the concierge's help, so he put on his sweat-absorbing shirt and bike pants and tied his runners. He made sure all his computers and tablets were logged off and then went to the elevator, which quickly centered his exhaustion and paranoia on the down button. He decided to walk first to the grocery store for his Red Bull, milk, and smoothie ingredients.

Downstairs he passed the concierge without nodding and went out to the visitor parking. Halfway to the footpath at the park entrance stood two dark-clothed figures of opposite sizes—a lanky male, an obese mass of indeterminate sex— who, when they started approaching Rick and tying bandanas over their mouths, wobbled with a frailty if not femaleness. Rick rapid-cycled through fatigue, dread, repulsion, violent possibility. As he walked nearer, broadening his angle so he wouldn't look scared if they were hostile, he reframed his thinking with deep assurances that these were just weird scenester people who'd been out all night and were making a rare appearance in the daylight. If it came to it, he was trained in Krav Maga and had a lawyer.

When Rick got close to them, they changed course to make up for his slight diversion. He walked past, bracing for confrontation. The big one jutted its elbow toward his shoulder. Rick leaped back and raised his fist and the woman kept coming. She took a swing and he pushed into her seal-blubber shoulder and retracted, avoiding escalation, unsure if he had the strength to move her or if there was any reason to do anything but walk away.

"Fuck you, Nazi!" hissed the skinny guy through double-rowed teeth. He quivered, gathering strength. "Don't touch her!"

The woman yelled, "Don't come near my body!"

Rick: "What the fuck do you want?"

"You fucking Nazi!" screamed the woman, eyes bovine and raging.

"Get away from me," said Rick, leaving, but the woman leapt at him, her stomach like a bag of Yukon Gold.

Rick took out his phone: "I'm calling the police."

The woman turned to lunge for it.

"What do you want? I'm calling."

"Fuck you, Nazi scum!"

Rick opened the dialpad.

"You're Heinrich Speer. You run a neo-Nazi site." The guy coughed. "Fuck you."

"I do a bit of work for a libertarian blog. Does that make me a Nazi?"

"Fuck you, Nazi! Germans can die!" she yelled with an ethnic flare.

"You're crazy," said Rick.

She screamed and a jogger coming from the park stopped, stared.

Rick pushed down with his hands as though getting to his feet. "You are *severely* mistaken." He appealed to the guy: "Do you know what you're doing? Who sent you to harass me? You should get a job. Because if any officer shows up and takes a look at you–"

"Is everything OK?" asked the jogger. She looked like Kathleen Wynne.

The female ANTIFA hesitated.

"Yes, everything is fine," Rick said. "I don't know who these people are."

"I have a recording of you on Nightrabbi! We have proof!"

a. beaumais

Rick's heart sped up, then his legs sped up. He turned and made for the condo buildings, pretending he was calling someone—the police—hoping the fat ANTIFA's word salad precluded any further interaction with the jogger, although the jogger's concerned Torontonian manner made this unlikely. He didn't look back.

It's happening: the leak in his opsec. Rick got in the elevator and slammed the wrong button, Floor 2. The door opened on Floor 2 and a man turned to board it going down, but Rick hit Floor 3 after the man hit Floor 1, so he went down again, the man smirking. The door opened on Floor 1 and Rick immediately pressed the button to close it, thinking he heard the concierge speaking in a loud voice.

When he finally got to his apartment, he locked himself in the bathroom and sat on the toilet lid. He had 13 new Twitter DMs. He knew what they were—knew this day had been preordained on the altar of time. A few days after Trump's victory, when the dissident right was feeling shock and momentum and something short of euphoria, he'd been invited by a Discord friend to appear on the Nightrabbi podcast. He'd declined, but the show had retweeted one of his articles on Ethereum smart contracts and he'd been deluged with pageviews. So, thinking a new world with a new God emperor was upon us and what the hell, he'd gone on the podcast anonymously, trying to artificially deepen his voice (the voice modulator he tried made him sound like Darth Vader), but he'd nonetheless left some breadcrumbs about his life and German sojourn, and when he'd begged Rhineland McDreams to take it down two weeks later, even offering the hipster-fascist $500, he'd refused.

Now.

dox

There was a smash. He left the bathroom and went onto the balcony. Two new black-clad ANTIFA had joined the first ones in the visitors' parking.

"You'll have to apologize to your neighbour on our behalf," yelled the skinny guy, holding his phone up to film.

"I'm calling security!" shouted someone from an upper floor.

"Tell them Rick Speer did it! Fuck Nazis!" shouted the girl.

Rick ducked back, away from the camera.

"What do you want?" he shouted.

"Delete your website! Show your face, Nazi fuck!"

His phone rang, his old normie friend's name flashing across the screen. He silenced it, and soon a text from Daryl appeared: "Your address is all over Facebook."

Fifty-eight notifications.

Black Bloc Scarborough'd posted a decade-old picture of his mother smiling beside his father at plates of salmon and salad-bedded potatoes awaiting them. For a split-second his head expanded like a distended watermelon, then he heard an Indian voice downstairs shouting at the ANTIFA. Rick's phone fell from his hands and the gorilla glass cracked. He could hear Ramesh haranguing them as his hands trembled and he reported, through the broken screen, the tweet with his mom's picture. He ran to the elevator. His mind was blank. He wanted to talk to his mother. Wanted to buy Ramesh a beer in a forked universe. The delay in the pain would end and the ruminations would unspool, the spidery paranoia. He realized he would kill himself. *No. No.* On the ground floor he ran into the overcast parking lot.

"This man is a neo-Nazi fascist," shouted a new

a. beaumais

ANTIFA in glasses.

Ramesh turned around and Rick took out his phone and tried to keep turned from any recording cameras. Ramesh looked like he was shooing a flock of geese.

"What are—"

"I'm calling the police," Rick shouted, dialling 911. "These people are harassing me and vandalizing the building. I don't know them but they're targeting my family."

"Fuck you, alt-right scum!"

The skinny ANTIFA came towards him. Rick stuck out a hand to block the filming.

Ramesh: "What are—"

"You're all going to get charged with vandalism, harassment, do you want me to go on?"

"Toronto Police," said a wiseguy voice.

Rick: "Officer, I'm calling to report vandalism, harassment, anti-social behaviour."

"What do you mean? Where are you?"

"There's a bunch of people dressed in black throwing rocks at my building. I'm at the condos at—"

"*No Nazis, no KKK, all fascists must pay. No Nazis, no KKK, all fascists must pay.*"

Skinny ANTIFA and glasses ANTIFA encircled him, spitting and slitting their throats like gangbangers.

"Where are you?"

"I'm trying to tell you. At the condoland at Lake Shore, 2–. Yes, that one. We're in the parking lot. My name is Rick Speer. Yes, this is my number!"

"Get out of here!" shouted Ramesh at all the geese.

The skinny one reached for Rick's phone and Rick swatted him in the ear. He staggered back like a pair of crutches.

"We're going to fucking end you," said the fat one. "See you soon."

They started dispersing in different directions, whether methodically or because they didn't know each other.

Rick gestured to Ramesh to hurry to the lobby.

"They broke the neighbour's window?" Rick asked. "I have no idea who they are. I'll pay the damages. I'm sorry to put you in the middle of this."

Rick heard himself from outer space—lobbying Ramesh maniacally—almost saw himself putting his arm around Ramesh's shoulder, imagined Ramesh throwing this arm off.

"Who are you?" said Ramesh, as they opened the lobby door.

"Rick Speer. Who are you?"

"Ramesh. But I'm asking, who *are* you?"

"I trade cryptocurrencies. I blog about blockchain. I had this strip–"

"I don't know," said Ramesh, knowing something Rick hadn't told him.

"I'll transfer you 3,000 for the windows."

"No, sir…"

"I'm doing it," said Rick, logging onto his mobile banking. "I feel responsible. I'm sorry for everything, I'm sorry."

A cop car pulled up slowly.

"Let me deal with this. Believe me. This is all my fault, but don't believe those things. They won't be back."

"Sir–"

Rick rushed through the door to meet the young officer, who looked Korean or Manchurian. *Park*, said the nametag. Rick reached out his hand, which Park regarded like a dead fish on a plate. When Rick withdrew it, the officer stuck his out. He shuddered.

"Thanks for coming."

"You're Rick Speer?"

"Yes."

"Where are these people?"

"They ran away. They're–" Rick held back a reactionary outburst.

"Where's the broken window?"

"It's upstairs. Both mine and my neighbour's. Someone who lives near me."

"Let's take a look."

This was all happening faster than Rick expected. He and Park took a few steps, rotating, Park waiting for Rick to lead the way. Rick felt like some member of an uncontacted tribe, unable to speak.

Rick moved slowly towards the door. He needed to get Park through the lobby without interacting with Ramesh, who he could see watching them behind the wiper-streaked windows. He needed to do a sweep of Twitter for doxxes to report. Then throw his laptop, clothes, bullion (where could he get a deposit box?), and pocket watch from Grandpa Ulf in a suitcase, head to the airport.

They went through the door and Ramesh rose at the front desk.

"Very grey sky," said Rick to Park, and then something about the windows that wasn't coherent, but Park didn't ask for clarification. They passed the baby grand and Rick looked over his shoulder to the front desk, tapping the up button. He shifted position to block Park's line of sight to the front desk, then went back to where he had been. Park looked at him.

dox

The elevator lit up and inside Rick slapped Floor 3 and ><.

"Sorry, I'm a bit shaken, to be honest."

Park swallowed. If Rick could escape to Daryl's, he could call his mother. He needed her words like a freezing agent on his heart. He had to decide where to flee. He started breathing faster and imagined himself diving out the window, Officer Park rushing down to the parking lot to find ANTIFA lording over his body resting in piss. It would probably not kill him to jump—they came out on his floor. Rick unlocked the door and Officer Park forged in without introduction, pulling out a Japanese knife on the kitchen island, inspecting the home theatre, the dust-caked PS4 and spaghetti cords, as if it was a meth lab. Rick flicked on the overhead light—almost turned it off again, boxers and takeout boxes awash on the rug.

He opened the last of the drapes for no reason.

Park found the rock on the counter, baseball-sized, rotated it as though appraising a gem.

"You think you're being targeted? Who are you—in your day-to-day life?"

"I work for a media company. I just do blogging—I mean, nothing. Really. Some day trading."

"Nothing? What's the blog?"

"*Free Speech?*"

"What's that?

"Austrian economics, that kind of thing, end the Fed."

"No, tell me, what *is* that?"

"It's an ideology about–"

"Anti-government? Do you sell anything?"

"No, it's more, I mean it's libertarian, anti–"

"Anti-state?"

a. beaumais

"Well. It's a libertarian blog."

"You mean anti-state ideology."

Rick sweated. He knew if he typed his name into Google he'd see the mother of all doxxes.

"Absolutely not. It's just about economic freedom and liberty."

Park opened the patio door and looked out onto the cars and the park.

"Did you see the people who did this?"

Rick thought. "Yes," he blurted. "I mean, barely. They looked like thugs. Like young kids." He hoped this didn't sound racist.

"Describe them."

He remembered the bandanaed large-limbed blubber. "They were wearing dark clothes. One was big, one was small."

He could not let on they were ANTIFA because this would implicate him. Even in the days after the election of Trump, when dissidents were still platformed, he would never have expressed his beliefs publicly—it was too hard to look Society in the eye. Now it was a hate crime.

"How many of them? Were they men?"

"I think two—one male, one female... a big female." He realized that Park was a small male.

He wondered whether he should start telling half lies or full lies. "I'm going to pay for the damages," he suddenly said. "I don't want to waste your time. You probably have better things to do."

Park smiled like a hunter whose game had giftwrapped itself in a trap.

"Won't your condo or your insurance pay for this? If

you had nothing to do with it. You sure you don't know these people? You hiding something?"

"No, sir," he said, "I mean, I don't know them."

There was silence blacking out everything he'd ever done.

Knock knock.

Rick looked at Park for permission.

As he went to the door, Rick thought of safe countries: Belarus, Thailand, Vietnam, Lichtenstein. Expecting Ramesh or another cop, he opened the door on a man with a big shaggy mustache, a ball cap, work boots, and a hospital-style shirt with a patch saying "McDowell."

"Heya."

"Hey."

"Got a broken window I hear."

"Yeah. Just back here," said Rick. "Officer Park is here. A police officer." He wondered if Park would notice that he'd noticed his name.

McDowell walked to the patio, throwing his hands up when he saw Park, as if he would fail a breathalyzer test and had oxies in his pocket but was claiming impunity as an honest tradesman.

Rick didn't know whether McDowell would help things or just add another spindle to his heartbeat. The man picked up a shard of glass and took his measuring tape to the window. Park looked between Rick and McDowell as though connecting the dots of conspiracy. Rick's phone pinged, pinged again. He stopped himself from looking as Park stared.

"This is your only address," said Park.

"Yes."

a. beaumais

Park exhaled: "Do you have an emergency contact?"

Rick gave him his mom's number.

He was sure this was leading up to something, but Park walked out, saying, "Give us a call if anything happens."

Rick only got more agitated, seeing the back of Park's police cap at the door. Park hadn't given him a business card or anything. Park would surely talk to Ramesh and learn that he was an Internet extremist. He wondered who'd been calling him as he opened the coat closet and yanked his suitcase from under a stack of shoeboxes. He ran to his dresser and swiped his grandfather's watch and a small, framed 18th-century map of Baden-Württemberg into it. He folded some pants and shirts and grabbed two pairs of shoes—remembered his passport, his eyedrops—before running into the kitchen with his half-open suitcase, almost clobbering McDowell.

"Woah!" McDowell said. "You're off quick."

"I found out my friend was in a car accident."

"Woosh. A'll get out of yer hair."

"Hm. Thanks."

"You run. I'll tell Rehar, uh, Hartree? Guy downstairs you had an emergency."

"No, please don't. I mean, it's OK. It wasn't so bad."

"Really?" McDowell's rosacea face dimmed. "Hm."

"Did Ramesh say anything about me when you came?"

"Well."

"Well?"

"Not exactly."

"Can you tell me," Rick said, picking up an undeposited cheque.

"I think he knows you're having a rough day."

"Are you not telling me something?"

"Look, I'm just the window guy."

"I'm sorry." Rick opened his wallet and gave him a 20.

"Really?" said McDowell.

"I appreciate your work."

"Didn't do nothing yet."

Rick tadpoled through the condo, casing his closet for his winter coat, toque, boots, almost putting them back right after, but what if he went somewhere cold? McDowell answered a 2G phone. Rick walked onto the balcony. Peered down slowly. Revealed more of the iceberg of people in the park, a golden retriever barking at a duck. Someone on a far bench, obscured by the water fountain and chlorophyll, black boots. Rick ducked back, leaned forward. He couldn't tell who it was, but when he poked his head a foot forward and looked down he saw the paddy wagon parked diagonally, like a dick. He didn't know if Park was in the car or in the lobby. He crouched smaller and opened Twitter. @SanFranciscoANTIFA 39m: "Lake Shore Blvd skinhead threatening LGBTQ2S and POC communities." He reported the tweet as abuse and reported two more that listed his address—three more—but more were popping up from avatarless accounts, one in Oklahoma, another located in "Your Screen," accounts with anarchist lightning-bolt symbols, a fat gamer named Carlos in Arizona, people who knew nothing about him, who'd never know him and yet were calling for his annihilation once removed. It was like he'd hit play on a Bach concerto and Ariana Grande was playing. He kept hitting Report, realizing how little credibility he had under the alias "The Wizard of Poz," which he quickly changed to "Wizard." Who was he kidding? The algorithm knew who he was and wanted him dangling from a rope. In a snap he deleted his Wizard of Poz account and start reporting the doxxes using his mostly unused Rick Speer account. He wondered if the doxxes reported under the Wizard of Poz would still get processed.

He stood up—crouched down again, seeing Park's cruiser. He dialled Daryl—got the answering machine. Time was mashing backwards like a tractor in a burnt field. He dialled again and Daryl grunted "yeah?"

"Hey, it's Rick. Sorry. Haven't talked in a while. I need to come to your house for a bit. I can't really explain. It's not safe. I'm not safe."

"What's going on? Your name is all over Facebook."

Rick looked back through a still-intact window, saw McDowell looking at him like his night-school JavaScript teacher sometimes did—trying to catch him up to some tricks. McDowell licked his lips and walked out onto the patio.

"I can't s–"

"That yer hurt bud?" asked McDowell.

Rick nodded, shook his head. Nodded.

McDowell cleared his throat and went inside to answer his phone.

"There are people after me," Rick whispered into his phone. "Outside my building. The cops are downstairs. I need to come to your place. Can I come to your place?"

"The fuck is going on? Why aren't the cops helping?"

He did not know how to circumnavigate Daryl's chad logic—the logic of a piano deliveryman. He would have to explain later.

"They are, sort of. But I need to leave here."

"Can you tell me what's going on?"

"I will later."

"You're a fucktard, Speer."

"I guess."

"So what are you doing?"

"I– I don't know." He wanted to cry. Wanted to hear his mother's voice.

"Do you need help getting out of there?"

Rick knew a forest he could hang himself in. He thought of the sushi knives in the kitchen. They could dice up a whole village of motherfuckers. He could do this. He stood up, the blood in his skull freefalling, and looked out upon the park, where he saw people in navy clothes by the fountain. "Yes."

"I'll be there soon."

"I'll tell you when to come."

"I'm coming now." Daryl hung up.

Rick looked down at the paddy wagon. He ran inside past McDowell to the bathroom, sunrays pinging behind his eyes. He clenched his jaw and collapsed on the toilet seat lid. He would need to get past Ramesh and Park. He texted Daryl: "don't come up. I'll come down." Needed to withdraw his money from the banks, two out of three of which would hold up anything bigger than 10K, needed to make ETC and BTC trades and find a way to launder USD, maybe with his friend in Cameroon, supposedly a Kotoko prince. They would freeze his accounts and smear him. Everyone would unfriend him and offer Freudian takes on his evil.

There was a knock on the bathroom door.

"Be back in 15," said the voice. "Going downstairs."

"Thank you. Thank you."

Cold sweat webbed through his temples and sideburns. He did not know who had done this—someone in his day-to-day life had heard him on Nightrabbi. Maybe one of his Internet friends had had a change of heart. It was always the stupidest explanation—the best friend, the aunt. Who had he spoken to recently? Ignored? He hardly had any friends except avatars on message boards, only three of whom knew his real name. Had Telia found something? Had he left his email open at her apartment? Had she gone through his phone while he was in the shower? Was this how she got his attention? He could not believe he was still talking to her. It couldn't be her. He opened the toilet, barfed water on a shit fleck. When he marched at the 13 Theses event the year before, he'd worn sunglasses and an arctic pilot cap and no one had posted his picture even after IDing almost all the marchers. His opsec had been formidable.

Rick stared down through his legs at the tiles, which needed caulking. He peered into the baby-blue ceramic. He could not adapt to the human stain. If anything, his reaction to modernity had not been rash enough, he decided. You either become soy and disappear, or you go down letting roman candles off in your enemy's face before they expunge you from history. The modern West was a bunch of ███ ████ ████ ████ ████ ████ ████, was it not? He started to feel better, a didactic pathway of his brain lighting up, as if he was lecturing the masses on moral philosophy in an amphitheatre. He punched the floor—it didn't matter if he could convince himself of his own beliefs.

He left the bathroom, remembering the suitcase. His terror made him stink. He began casing the apartment for anything valuable.

"I'm downstairs," pinged a message from Daryl.

He went out on the patio. The paddy wagon was gone. He put on a fedora and aviators and zipped up his suitcase. When he opened the door McDowell was stepping out of the elevator. He almost tried to pretend McDowell, staring at him, was not there. But then he took off his hat and sunglasses when they got close.

"Eh, you."

"I left it unlocked. I need to see my friend. Maybe Ramesh can lock up later."

"I'll ask him. Hey, I wanted…"

"What?" asked Rick.

"Nah, it's OK."

Rick was already in the elevator, heart pincered by a thousand tiny crabs.

In the lobby he skipped past Ramesh, who he heard on the phone saying, "I spoke to the man…"

Rick came out under the cloudy sky and saw Daryl staring at him in his GMC, with revulsion maybe, or maybe he didn't recognize him, till Rick waved. Daryl slowly reached for the auto-unlock. Rick lobbed his suitcase into the backseat, almost grazing Daryl.

"The hell are you wearing?"

"Can we leave?"

"What'd you do?"

"Let's get out of here. Seriously."

"Talk to me. Take a breath."

Rick took off his hat and sunglasses, looked around. The world was foreclosed and in his phone.

"People are hunting me," he said after a few seconds. "ANCOMs, antifascists, whatever. I don't even care about politics."

"What?"

Rick forgot that Daryl interpreted the world in terms

of Netflix and the NFL rather than left–right.

"Please just drive. Insane left-wing freaks are trying to kill me."

"Where? Here?"

"Yeah."

"I want to see these people."

"Dude. If you don't drive I'm going to leave."

"Stop pissing yourself."

Rick wiped the gel crust under his fedora as Daryl put the car in drive, did a three-point turn. A man walked a Weimaraner outside the Metro grocery store. They waited to turn left at the stop sign. Rick stared into the park. The two black bloc stood a few feet away—five metres, tops—and Rick slunk in his seat, evaporating like a witch.

Daryl stopped the car and looked at Rick. "What? Is that them?"

The car behind them honked.

"Deal with this. Like a fucking *man*." Daryl reached for the handle.

"No! Seriously. Don't do this."

Daryl opened the door as honking cars started to go around them. Rick slouched at the bottom of the seat, treading time, remembering an afternoon playing *Counterstrike* with Daryl. Rick waited 10 seconds and inched his head up to see Daryl wildly gesticulating at the ANTIFA, the skinny guy, the fat woman yelling, teeth gnashing under her hoodie. He texted Daryl to come back and peered outside the car as though out of a space pod. Daryl looked at his phone and then back at the car. Daryl started walking back, waving the black bloc towards him.

They came to the door. Rick slowly got out of the

car, keeping his face turned in case they were recording.

"They're saying you're a neo-Nazi."

"They're mistaking me for someone. I already told them. They broke my window and the police were here."

"Do you hear this?"

"He's lying," said the skinny ANTIFA.

"He's a fucking white supremacist!"

Daryl smiled, looked back at Rick and then at the black bloc. "Hm. Get outta here. You guys look bored."

The fat one charged forward and by the time Rick got his arm up he was getting kicked in the shin. He fell against the car door and slunk, hopping, feeling a smooch of blood under the skin. Daryl shoved the fat ANTIFA and she jerked forward, climbing stairs in the air like a crying tree. Daryl dodged as the skinny one threw a yellow water bottle that exploded in a rain of piss on the car, wetting Rick's sole. Daryl stepped to the skinny black bloc, who reached in his black paper-bag jeans and threw something small and metallic, denting the window. A battery rolled under Rick. The skinny one threw up his hands and turned his head away and Daryl's fists pummelled his bony forearm till Rick said, "Let's go!"

Daryl moved toward the car, and Rick saw the skinny one's hood come off, revealing a GoPro band dangling from his ripped hood.

"He's been recording."

"What?" said Daryl, opening the car door.

"He has a GoPro."

An elderly couple idled in their sedan, watching. The anarchist blob gathered strength and stood to her feet like a meat-injected giraffe.

"We need to take it," Rick said.

a. beaumais

"Fucking take it then!"

Rick ran to the prone, skinny black bloc and reached his hand out as if to a crippled animal, *Please bear with me.* He reached for the GoPro and the skinny guy squealed like he was robotripping and snapped at Rick's finger and bit him. Rick pulled back his hand and looked at the bloody crater of skin as Daryl backhanded the skinny one in the neck and yanked the GoPro from his forehead. They got in the car as the fat girl sobbed. Rick bled over his shirt and pants. When Rick turned around, he saw Ramesh standing outside the lobby doors.

They drove.

"Don't get it on the seats," said Daryl, shifting into third.

*

They parked outside Daryl's bungalow in Old East York and went through his garage full of Suzuki motorcycle parts, plasma cutters, rags. Daryl'd told Rick he could lay low in the basement, and Rick wanted to retreat there to call his mother, but Hannah intercepted them at the garage door in an apron, holding a hamper of white, warm-looking towels.

"Oh. Oh! What happened?" she cried, grabbing him by the arm. She brought him to a tiny bathroom whose door opened from the inside and made it impossible for them to both fit. "Keep your hand over the sink," she said, and left. He needed stitches but they couldn't sew his identity back together. He reached into his pocket for his phone, but it wouldn't unlock with his right thumbprint and his left hand was leaking.

"What happened to you guys?"

Hannah snapped open a first-aid kid.

"I don't know," Rick said, his voice foreign. "There were these people outside my apartment."

"Who?"

He was lightheaded and starved. "I don't know."

His brain was decaffeinated and gauze-stuffed, his words like ketchup and mustard stains in napkin folds.

"We should take you to the hospital," she said.

"No, can we just wrap this up."

Hannah took his head lightly and peered into his eyes, scanning his sclera, his pupils, his reaction times, looking down to his hair and jeans, performing a battery of cognitive motherly tests. "I don't know if you're thinking clear, Rick. I don't know what my husband is thinking either. You're not telling me something."

Rick's mind was a Tinder app finding all the *I don't knows* within three kilometres. "I'm sorry. Honestly. You're always so wonderful."

She applied iodine to the finger and Rick cringed, waiting for the fire to die out, embers that would burn for many nights. Usually, in a tired state like this (not even counting the wound), he'd be planning a nap in order to regain a few IQ points, but he didn't know what to do now besides live out the opposite of a nap and stare at Hannah, who'd put on a few pounds since the last time he saw her but, if anything, was more alluring, with cherry-red lips. She covered the wound with gauze and medical tape, saying something again about the hospital.

"I'll think about it. I promise." He followed her out and she opened the door to the basement. He went downstairs, looking back at her looking at him. He sat on the linty green couch he'd picked at compulsively when it was at Daryl's parents' and they'd play PlayStation 2. He touched his phone, a piñata of flags. His heart ticked separate from his body. His words kept autocorrecting. Telia'd called four times. He typed an extended message ending in, "*While I treasure all our time together, I need some time alone in order to deal with my issues, including these bizarre accusations that I can assure you are fabricated.*" He paused before hitting Send—did he need her? He left it as a draft, seeing 17 new messages in his inbox, three from Telia. One from Bela, but it was blank. Most of the emails were from *Free Speech* interns and a one-time co-author at *Hate Facts* who he'd become estranged from after an argument about optics ("are IQ arguments beyond the Overton window… do we need trailer-park people in our movement?"). On Twitter, some doxxes about the Lake Shore Blvd. skinhead had been scrubbed, but now a CTV reporter named Sammy Phelps was replying to people for details—was in all likelihood in contact with the black bloc outside his condo. He wished he'd taken the klonopin from his apartment. Sooner or later, some good Samaritan would tip off the police. If ANTIFA knew about his involvement with *Hate Facts*, there'd be new pressure to shut down the PayPal accounts, which were still open through a miracle of God. If *Free Speech* found out he'd written for *Hate Facts* (it was mostly Marvin Myers III who didn't know), they'd fire him for starters. Maybe they'd leak the details of his forex business and the massage parlor/strip club BBS.

He lay on the couch, checkmated, sublimating the searing in his hand in the screaming in his brain as he heard the pinging of another text. Another. Another. He breathed—another. His mind spun the yin and yang of Telia and Bela, his phone pinging till he opened his eyes and violently grabbed it. It flew from his bum fingers to the shag carpet. He picked it up, shouting, "Haven't you done enough already?" But then he thumbprint-unlocked it and read the newest SMS:

1) This is a dox.

2) You, Rick Speer, appeared on the Nightrabbi podcast as a bitcoin expert and the shownotes provided Twitter handle @Wizard_of_Poz_0.

3) Wizard of Poz admitted on July 21st in a screenshotted Discus comment to being an editor-at-large of Hate Facts.

4) The voice on the Nightrabbi podcast matches that of Rick Speer on Oct. 21 of the previous year on CBC Radio.

Rick bit down on his tongue, gasped ratlike. He'd always known—the leak in his opsec would sink him. One day. He wanted to scream—it would have been an underreaction—but he just whimpered and shook in a dry, jester-like way. He lapped up iron in his gums. *Ping. Ping.*

5) The CBC program was about Oktoberfest. On Dec. 4 of last year and Mar. 1 of this year, two Hate Facts-affiliated Facebook accounts made cryptic mention of you attending Oktoberfest and you responded affirmatively.

Was there a bathroom down here?

He'd been leaving Oktoberfest at midnight at the Kitchener Concordia Club and on the way to the taxi, a CBC reporter put a microphone in his face, *Can I ask what Oktoberfest means to you?* expecting some gay platitude shit, and he was too drunk and sad to not act out, so he said, "All the beer halls from Kitchener to Munich and all the way to the Volga are toasting Frederick II and what it means to be children of the Rhine, the intractable bond of the volk." The reporter was confused and he repeated this in German.

Her suspicion was conciliated by his laser-like expression. He remembered what he'd been thinking that night—obsessing over a dark-haired girl named Klara from Brandenburg—her kiwi shampoo, her high nasal bridge—who'd gone cold-fish on him at a Vietnamese restaurant after she glimpsed her ex-boyfriend through the window—tall, hard-wired tropical Aryan phenotype. That Oktoberfest, he couldn't hold a conversation with his friend (who hadn't talked to him since), but managed to show the friend many pictures of the ex-bf as he contemplated his poverty and Canadian deficiencies, his movie trailer of social anxieties.

A teardrop had slipped down his radioactive cheek. He wanted to call his mother, to go back to childhood, the basement, the womb. *Ping.*

6) We demand nothing short of the deletion of Hate Facts; otherwise, this thread, with full documentation, will be circulated to all major news outlets.

The door opened. When Rick decided to lift his head, he saw Daryl, agitated—they were both agitated—mouth tremoring, rehearsing.

"So tell me what the fuck just happened."

Rick took a breath: "I run various websites. Some of the content is kind of out there. Nothing violent–"

"When are you going to be out of here?"

"Let me finish."

Daryl had murder in his eyes.

"Somehow my identity was leaked. And deranged freaks are coming for me."

"And why the fuck didn't you get the police to deal with it? And you still didn't say when you were going to leave."

"Because our society–"

"What!"

"Our society is fucked up."

"What the fuck is wrong with you?"

"Do you want me to leave?"

"Finish your sentence." Daryl paced to his DVD tower.

"I don't have faith in law enforcement to not investigate me for some kind of fucking hate crime or freeze my bank accounts."

"My brother is a fucking cop."

"I know. It's not all cops. But I don't know what I'm going to do. Someone is threatening–"

"You! I don't care about your problems. How does it affect me? Do these people know where you are? Swear, if these people come near my daughter, I'm going to cut your throat open with a skate."

"As far as I know–"

"Fuck you!"

"As far as I know they have no idea who you are. Unless they videotaped us."

"But we took the–the–"

"GoPro."

"Yes. Fuck you."

"So it shouldn't be an issue unless someone else was recording."

"Shouldn't be? I'll tell you what. Shouldn't be an issue for you to fuck off outta here in the next 20 minutes."

Rick looked at him sternly—it was all he could do—all the tree roots of their childhood bonds liquefying, returning to their previous non-existence, never-existence. He had better friends scattered throughout the world, but he'd assumed Daryl would back him in some big-brother way.

a. beaumais

"You gonna answer me?"

"I'll be gone in the next 45 minutes."

"OK," he barked.

"OK."

Daryl left him in the basement.

His drug fog was dissipating, revealing the scorched flowers of fatigue like a shrine in a blown-out door. *Life comes at you fast.* In the hierarchy of recent surprises—the dox, the Pomeranian's basement, the MDMA—Daryl's betrayal did not rank high. He stared at the brick wall, his vision skipping leftward in rapid spurts, a serotonin tic, the survival drive tapdancing through his ribcage. He typed his thoughts in a MemoPad:

```
technically could delete site.
But should not ?
berger and Quandt would know it was me
talk to them? transfer money?
Barbados, Cayman Islands
```

He couldn't delete the site—the founders, one of whom knew his name and address, or former address now, would not close the only remaining highly trafficked NRx site over an ANTIFA witchhunt—the whole point was to hold your ground till the day CloudFlare cut you off, till the day the feds blacklisted your bitcoin address and fed you to the sharks. These people wouldn't care if he got doxxed. Anyone in dissident politics after the cosmic belly flop of Donald Trump already lived like a centipede under the mattress, perpetually swatted at and losing limbs. Most were estranged from their families let alone their neighbours, and there was no going back—you could drop off your daughter at kindergarten and shop at the farmer's market all you wanted, there was no way of unlearning the truth when the reason you learned it in the first place was you were a sad failure.

If he deleted the site, the dox would still bubble up in archived posts and screenshots, and the whole *Hate Facts* and *Free Speech* mastheads would declare a fatwa against him and could do more damage than ANTIFA and law enforcement combined.

If he didn't delete the site, the dox would continue. Checkmate.

…

His hand selected his mother's contact and hit Call. He hadn't talked to her in two months. Didn't know what was new with her in retirement. Was she seeing anyone? Did she know anyone with a gun?

"How have you been."

He didn't say anything. He started to cry away from the receiver, slapped himself and clawed his face. "Hi Mom."

"Is everything okay?"

His thoughts flitted to *Hate Facts*, to the SMS stream. He wanted to look at his messages, wanted to tell her he'd call her back.

"Hello?"

"Hey… Yeah, I'm okay. Just a little tired."

"How's Telia?"

"We're kind of on the rocks."

"Are you going to work things out?"

She was clueless—Telia was a vacant beehive in the outer ring roads of yesterday—but, rather than say this, he said maybe and listened to her breathing, tumbling through the vacuum of it, the phantom umbilical cord, imagined being submerged in pre-existence like a bottle of pink champagne in a poolside ice bucket in the summer, or, better yet, never to have existed.

"We should do something, Mom."

"That's what I always say, but you never call."

"What are you doing today?" he said.

"I'm planting bulbs. And I'm expecting Margerie anytime."

"OK. Maybe I'll call you again soon."

"I hope you do."

He hung up before she could ask anything, her voice singing in his cerebellum like a jukebox on fire. A staticky dial tone in his brain. He did not want to commit suicide because he didn't want to see blood spurt from his wrists, or feel regret in the second before dying, or know for sure that his life had never mattered. He had places he could flee to. Tomas? His best friend from primary school had moved to Japan at 23 to teach English, where he congregated with Internet women in mall bathrooms for zipless fucks before settling down with Kimi and becoming a Yanoi larper who didn't have Japanese citizenship. Rick was too old to learn pictograms, was too much of a hulking clumsy white man, even with black hair and ghost-blue skin, to embed himself among them. His one other friend had married a rich Montreal yenta and converted and was too handtied by his brood of kids to do anything.

Rick realized how smart his friends had been to further their haplogroups, eat three meals a day, 9-to-5 mimetic life, family dog—even if they never recoded the fabric of history. It's not like anyone did outside a couple scientists and war criminals. Most people who changed history were just petty mutations like the Trumps, snake-oil salesmen, butchers, sex-addicted prophets—everything playing out according to steam engines in the stratosphere set in motion billions of years ago.

He scrolled the tectonic pileup of notifications on Twitter—an organism exhaling CO_2. He started deleting posts from his personal Twitter account as though ripping plants out of a carefully tended garden. When they were gone he felt none of the loss he'd expected, but a small ephemeral relief, like a child throwing sand out of his pockets into the sea. He locked the account. He'd delete it later. He thought of Bela and how he'd been a piece of shit to her—pictured her in a boggy woodland at dusk, wearing a white robe, lilies in her hair: she looked into a hand mirror and the reflection was that of a wrinkled, snow-haired, regal lady, five decades into the future.

He had to speak to her again, say sorry. All he wanted was for her to acknowledge he was sorry: he felt certain, almost, that if she acknowledged his feelings towards her, it would boost her self-worth one percent, and that would be enough for him to walk in front of a train.

He looked at his Gallery, at a selfie he'd taken of himself and Bela last night on the couch. Smiling the kind of cathartic smile that only breaks through in the middle of the night in the middle of a teenage summer—a smile he'd only ever seen in his dreams.

13 Theses popped up in an SMS on his screen. A scent-linked memory of that day stormed overhead. He clicked the message.

7) We also have reason to believe that you were one of the four men yet to be identified who participated in the 13 Theses March. We're so confident, in fact, that if you don't delete Hate Facts, we will, after

a. beaumais

publicizing our findings, promptly collect the $10,000 reward offered by the Rudderman Foundation.

His heart skipped like a CD player. He'd worn such a thorough disguise, so hobolike and mocking, that his fellow marchers couldn't identify him. Hadn't even paid attention to the post-march crackdown and trail of doxxes, besides reading about the guy from Ann Arbor who committed suicide. He stretched his neck farther sideways than it had ever gone. The dust spun like a slot machine. Who the fuck was behind this? An Internet extremist graduate program. Southern Poverty Law Center. ANTIFA. Some random trap coder he'd offended some random Tuesday morning.

He had no choice.

"I'm being blackmailed," he wrote in the *Hate Facts* Slack. "they demand that I delete the site."

"Hold your ground," said Pokie, a Colombian 23-year-old, within seconds.

"These people will get me killed."

Raymond: "What do they have on you?"

"They found out about Oktoberfest and the march."

"Hah. just ignore them. thats the only way to deal with them."

"They've sent people to my condo."

"sorry to hear that. u need 2 lay low for a little while. responding to them will only make it worse. we cant delete the site. that would only things worse & u know it. we have a mission. im sorry."

Rick: "Let's take it down for a week. Long enough for me to get on a plane somewhere."

"no. were not going to negotiate with basement dwellers"

Rick didn't respond. He closed Slack, paced the

room. He had to leave. He went to the DVD tower and back, thinking about these freaks he'd spent so many sleepless nights talking to—how they appealed to the "mission"—as if it was some yellow-brick road to a cloud-laden nirvana of ideology, as if the rocks coming through his window were no heavier than the morning paper. These were digital nomads gathered around a burning tire, spit-roasting memetic rats, waiting for some fucking dictator to save them, circle-jerking their circumcised pricks to whatever 4D-chess move Trump'd just lost the plot doing. All the best ones had left years ago.

It was time.

There was no hope for these people, whose rejection of shibboleths was due as much to their poverty of skills and volcanic minds—minds that stopped them from creating parallel institutions without devouring each other, let alone thriving in the current ones—as any Spenglerian historicism.

He'd write something back to them later, maybe. He'd always known they were like this, they'd given so many signs that they would let him down in ways he could not understand, or even talk to normal people about. He imagined trying to describe them to Daryl—*Oh, the guys I work with? This one Hate Facts editor-at-large apparently has a 150 IQ, but no one's ever heard his voice except a programmer in his hometown in Maine he plays RTS games with. And some people say this editor is actually a gay guy in a village in India… And this fiber-optic millionaire covering payroll at Free Speech has some really good ideas on using mailing lists to boost our reach. But he always brings up that he's never had a girlfriend and I can literally see Chunky soup stains on his clothes. He's pretty good-looking and he's obviously rich so I don't get it. They sound weird? Oh I know, I work with them and they're pretty smart, but… I mean, I haven't met them in person. I don't know.*

a. beaumais

These were the men who, though not maintaining relationships with anyone besides the mailman and a pet snake, excoriated others for their bad social skills. These were the last men standing up for the hairy beating heart of identity.

His brain puked. He tied his shoes dizzily, his brow milking. He needed to lie down but he wondered if fixing himself was worth it. Step one: get out of here. He plugged the house number into Uber and hoisted his suitcase up step by step with his unmaimed hand, opened the front door and found himself on the stoop with a few seconds left before he could faint. All the blood was funnelling out of his head into his toes. He turned around, decided to say goodbye like an embarrassing drunk uncle, but he heard a click and saw Daryl's silhouette through the lace curtain.

A Honda Civic pulled up, probably the driver's, and he opened the door upon a man with a shiny head like a genie's. The man apologized for his giddiness. "It's a great day, my friend. For my brother had a baby." "Where's your brother?" "Islamabad, friend." As they passed lawn gnomes on Mortimer Avenue, Rick could not drum up anything better than "oh, nice," though under his Jurassic sediment of unpersonhood he sensed some kind of wind of caring, some worthiness in exchanging platitudes, in recycling the oxygen for his fellow man. He closed his eyes and before long was hearing "Sir? Sir?" having less fallen asleep than entered an insect state where he drew minute breaths and inhabited the timescale of a mollusc fossil in a lake.

They were already in Rosedale among big red bricks, everything—the dox, the Ogóreks, the Pomeranian, Daryl, the broken glass—having the quality of a nightmare that was about to dissipate and leave a bad aftertaste, an SSRI gone wrong. "Good luck with the baby," he said, getting out. "I mean, your brother."

He wheeled the suitcase up the Ogórek pathway, the veins in his hands rising like bread. He rang the doorbell, which he expected didn't work, looking side to side from the wild shrubs to the disused bird feeder stained with algae and duck shit. To his right were the curtains drawn at the Pomeranian's. He hadn't rehearsed what he was going to say, had been thrown from the magic cortical carpet onto the coals of testosterone. He felt like his confidence would be bolstered in his appeals to Bela if he went to the bank and withdrew a thick stack, to be used with a gun to his head in a romantic threat that would underwrite him with fatalism. In his mental state he was naked.

He heard a scurrying inside. He stood straighter and breathed.

Jane answered the door in her mermaid mask.

She slammed the door shut. He knocked again. Nothing. He stepped back down the stoop onto the pathway: looked up. On the top floor a window was open, the ivied trellis almost colonizing it. He wondered if Mr. Ogórek was lying in that little cubicle of the sky. Rick wanted to call out, but Mr. Ogórek, if he was not in the hospital, would be in no form to answer the door. A crow crowing in a tree eclipsed the sun, orange-blue rays sizzling through branches. A dog woofed. Rick strayed on the lawn towards the Pomeranian's. One of the windows had a neon-lettered For Sale sign. Squinting, his eyes could not see any gaps in the blinds, any lurkers. The sun splashed and liquefied his vitreous; he felt that it was wrong to loiter facing that way, even if he was living in a kind of after-life—felt that there was evil in that house, that that man was ancient and evil, that for centuries his spirit had lived in these fields haunting children and small farm animals. He thought of 4chan and almost vomited, like having a bad song in your head during a hangover. He hurried back to the Ogóreks' door, sprinting as though to crash through the window and protect Jane, a human shield against the Pomeranian. He decided that the Pomeranian had fled, or was barricaded and armed deep in his dark room. The cops hadn't called him about last night.

He stood on the Ogórek porch and dialled Bela— told her answering machine there was a For Sale sign next door, trying with his tone to sound boy-next-doorish and not referencing the last part of last night's conversation at Loft404, which would set him back to zero by any measure.

He knocked again, *duh duh duh-duh duh… duh duh.* Jane opened the door as if this was the right password. She stared and gave an eyeroll (uncharacteristic of her lack of body language) that said, "Are you coming in or not?" He entered, aware of the optics of bad men and young girls, but far beyond giving a fuck about fuck. The old-wood smell in the foyer. If someone touched him he'd drop like a feather. It felt like he'd been here weeks ago as opposed to yesterday.

"Where's your sister?"

"Hmm."

"Bela."

"Not here."

"Where? Where'd she go?"

"To the puh-*lease.*"

"Where's your da– daddy?" He felt strange using this phrase and stuttering, as if it stamped the pedo vibes.

"Having a dream."

dox

"Is he OK?"

She ran into the kitchen, and he thought she was going to bring him something—a doctor's note, a phone number—but she just started humming. He shut the front door and entered the den, sunrays casting sepia rainbows on the hardwood. Family photos and old glories. *A flower can't bloom forever.* Their mother in a trench coat holding an umbrella over her wavy ashen hair. A painted orca. A grandpa holding a French loaf in Paris. Good genes, he thought. He wanted to stay here. There was something sheltering about the room, like a crypt blooming with flowers. It reminded him of a videogame he'd played as a kid, something about the city of Midgar—an ambient chill diffused down his spine. He would have gladly gone back to childhood, playing all-night sessions in the dark with the CRT monitor blow-drying his tear ducts.

He remembered his phone but couldn't bear to look. He just wanted to sit here in the dust. He could hear Jane humming. She was, when you wiped the candy off her face, the most beautiful daughter, with the Instagram neoteny of a child actor, rosy cheekbones and snub nose, the ability to deliver lines as a heart-rending meme. He would put her in his will.

His phone buzzed with a call. Daryl.

"Hello?"

"Fucking scum posted the fucking video! My face on the Internet on fucking YouTube?"

"Wait, say that ag–"

"Fuck you! Fuck you!"

"What's on YouTube?"

"The video. Of me!"

"Where?"

a. beaumais

"Fucking YouTube!"

"Send me the link."

"I'll fucking end you!"

Daryl hung up.

Rick received a link to a hyper-pixelated YouTube video of the parking-lot scene. Rick watched it two, three times. His head was obscured for basically all of it, due to crouching off-camera. But there was a point, when the battery hit the car, where the lens zoomed in with its shitty 240p and caught Daryl's profile, which, if not immediately identifiable, would be with a touch-up, crowdsourced on a message board.

The uploader was "TORONTO IRON FIST /22/."

Rick logged in under one of his sock accounts and wrote, "The tall guy had nothing to do with it. Take down the video and I'll send you $5000 on PayPal." He deleted this comment, saying *son of a fuck*, which Jane parroted in the other room, when he realized it could open him to people copying the video and blackmailing him. He found TORONTO IRON FIST /22/'s Twitter in the "About" section. He DM'ed them, raising the stakes to $8K—his duty to Daryl wrenching him from his honeymoon with obliteration. He started coughing as though to purge all life. His heart pinched and he got up to outrun it—ran to the steps outside. The thought of a chain reaction taking down Daryl was heinous—not because he liked Daryl, but because the whole thing was so farcical the way modernity was—a piano mover facing mob violence for his non-friend's thought crimes on the Internet.

On Twitter, TORONTO IRON FIST /22/ DM'ed him: "We will take it down for 2 hrs. you have that long to deliver us funds… 10,000. we already have people identifying this individual."

dox

The front door opened behind Rick, then shut. He turned and saw Jane in the sunroom window, reclined like a gazelle. Something about her taunted and irritated him. He thought about calling the police and telling his story in a blank, sterile room to a sympathetic beat cop with a cattle-herder haplogroup and a history of family alcoholism who'd accept him as a sophisticated currency trader who'd gotten in with rough characters. Rick could offer tips (lies) on black-box trades and the Silk Road. But no—if the cop searched *Hate Facts* and saw it on the SPLC list, there was no telling what this could lead to—sensitivity training, community service, frozen bank accounts, jail, no-fly list. All for what? A police escort for a few hours? A larpy cop who'd say, "I loathe what you say but I'll defend to the death your right to say it," only to ruin his life? The police could sort out the dox no more than Nerds On Site could fix his router. The dox would linger in archive sites like a Herpes simplex. All he could do was put cortical cream on it.

He DM'ed TORONTO IRON FIST /22/: "Can you meet in Chorley Park in the next few hours?"

"thatll require an extra $500 in fees."

"Fine."

"actually extra $1000."

He had C$92K in the bank, a paid-off condo, hard drives of BTC and Ethereum, C$21,000 in bullion and Spanish coins, US$23,500. The problem was how to move what was in the banks. If the dox stayed in the form of screenshots of his name and address, or a hit piece on *ItsGoingDown* linking him to *Hate Facts*, he might be able to change his name and respawn somewhere. But if he was revealed as a 13 Theses marcher, it would get on the news and they'd throw the book at him and feed him to the sharks. He could convert his savings into bitcoin, but it might crash. He could put his condo up for sale, but there was no time. He could transfer his savings offshore, though he'd need to find someone who could stuff it away fast. Maybe his money would be untouched, maybe he'd just get banned from PayPal and put on a no-fly list—but who needed to go to the USA anyway?

A light shaft belched from the clouds, forming a spotlight on the needle-bedded pathway. He had to make amends. He looked at his phone, at the carefully punctuated text messages from the unknown number.

"I cannot delete Hate Facts," he texted the mysterious number. "It isn't my site. I can offer you $15K and my personal resignation from the Internet in return for you helping to bury the 13 Theses allegations and doing anything you can to stem the dox."

"We will not negotiate with Nazis under any circumstances," said The Number.

Rick wondered if the "we" was a lie or if he was dealing with a distributed network.

"I have no means to delete the site. I'm not an admin."

"You have 24 hours to delete Hate Facts if you don't want your involvement in the 13 Theses march publicized."

He went to https://www.hatefacts.org/login but couldn't remember his username and password. For the last few months they'd used a Fiverr factchecker from Azerbaijan to glance over the articles before publishing, and Rick thought that the Azerbaijani's password was the same as his with the addition of two characters—was sakhld!@#!@#hareds or more like sakhld!@#!@#hare33. He tried four different combinations. He checked his phone to see if The Number

dox

had messaged him. He felt the chemicals in his brain gurgling, both sides of his skull copulating as the dregs of MDMA forged ghost connections. Neuropathic stress patterns were being etched that would create compulsions for weeks—he plucked three hairs from the crown of his head.

He shook.

"All okay?" A postman appeared on the sidewalk with a stack of letters atop a yellow Amazon package.

When Rick didn't reach out, the mailman put the mail in the mailbox, flyer-stuffed and missing its top. Rick took three breaths, trying to iron out his brainwaves and shit the password.

sakhld!@#!@#hareds
sakhld!@#!@#har3ds
sakhld!@#!@#Hareds

The page started loading and he felt a wave of gratitude. He had to do this. He'd get doxxed very thoroughly and excommunicated by all these people but at least he wouldn't be unmasked as a 13 Theses Marcher—unless *Hate Facts* did this. Maybe he could just delete his own articles. But then The Number would know he had admin power. OK, he would change the passwords, take the site down, and flee to Moldova, his money trailing a couple days behind, apologizing to *Hate Facts* and writing "404" on the homepage. He'd tell Pokie that he'd give the keys to the site back as soon as he reached safety, and he would, and they'd hate him, but they'd never have to see him, and probably wouldn't sabotage things before he restored the site.

OK: screw it: *Let's do this.*

As a test, he tried to hide one of his old posts. He hit Unpublish.

a. beaumais

You must be an administrator to perform this action.

He tried a different post.

You must be an administrator to perform this action.

Jane opened the door and sat beside him on the step, running her hands through his hair, conducting electricity in his skull. He looked at her and thought to kidnap her. Not because he wanted to, but just because that was what you were expected to do as a bad man. He was bad—he had the value to society of someone who would abduct a little girl.

"I have just tried to delete the site," he typed to The Number with Jane's hands in his hair. "It's impossible."

He did not get a response and wrote, "25K cash. Meet me in Toronto. Please. I am ruined. I will check in with you every few weeks. I'll prove I haven't been involved with Hate Facts. I will talk to anyone. If you link me to the March, you will sic a violent mob on me."

"You are my enemy," said The Number, changing its pronoun. "There is no moral judgment attached to harming you."

"Give me 48 hours to delete it," said Rick. "I can't do it in 24. You're forcing me to commit violence against these people. They live nowhere near me and I need to somehow threaten them?"

He received an MMS: a "Death" Tarot card with a horseback skeleto-knight riding up on a yellow bishop. He noticed the U.S. spelling of "color." He knew there was no point threatening anyone at *Hate Facts*. He wondered whether there was some place you could go to surrender, some neighbourbood for the unpersoned where you could trade all your wealth and freedom to live in a fully automated luxury open-air prison where they wouldn't get you. Some place for all the #MeToo men, Jeffrey Epstein's pedophile island, some place where you ate tapas by the pool, because even if your reputation was fish food, it's not like your money was.

Jane went inside and he felt his skin crawling, the sky watching, cameras and satellites trained on him. *The invention of photography is the greatest disaster of the 20th century*, according to Bernhard. He turned off his phone and shivered. He couldn't calm down. He needed to flee the cameras, sensors, cell towers, Google trackers. He went inside and downstairs to the basement, Jane trailing. Found himself in the cold cellar, wine bottles lining the wall, the basement crypt smell. Shards of glass drizzled with blood. This must have been where Ron fell. He could not believe no one had cleaned up. But then he believed it, trawling the floor with his shoe for glass and sitting against the wall, the coolness of the earth breathing through the concrete. He put his head in his hands, bending forward to blink out the world. He hallucinated Ron's face. He sat up and said, "Is your dad okay?"

"Sleeping."

"Is he hurt?"

"Yes."

"Can I see him?"

She didn't say anything.

"Can I see him?"

"Kay."

He did not know if he'd be welcomed by Ron, but he had to apologize for mistreating his daughter, for breaking into the Pomeranian's, for not being Polish. He wanted to pledge fealty and offer himself up. Ron wouldn't give a fuck about the dox.

They went upstairs to street level, and Jane led the

way to the second floor. Rick wondered if the Ogóreks had been rich in the Old World. There were paint chips on the stairs to the third floor and the railing popped out of the hinges.

They stopped outside what Rick assumed was Ron's room. Rick peered through the crack in the door and entered.

It smelled terminally stale. The lace curtains were open and the sun streamed over the cold dank. Ron lay on the bed in a jean jacket, a red molten goose egg on his head. The old box TV, an Eaton Viking, was tuned to a muted infomercial. A half-drunk 26'er of Żubrówka vodka sat on the bedside table beside a crossword puzzle and a Mrożek novel.

"Ron, it's me. Rick Speer."

Ron blinked at the ceiling.

"Do you remember me?"

Ron closed his mouth mostly and did not speak. Jane jumped on the bed and his leg dropped like quicksand into the gap between two mattresses pushed together. She said something in Polish and after a few seconds he said something back—like a refrain or automated response.

"Hello," said Rick.

Ron spoke to Jane, but the words were like a flashlight sputtering out, a starved bat flapping against a drainpipe. In looking inward, Rick always forgot that time was sapping those around him.

Rick took out his phone and dialed Bela. Maybe he should bring Ron to the hospital. The sun beat through an opaque windowpane into the black-hole room. He got the answering machine: *Bela, I'm with your father at your house. He is not...* Rick stepped into the hall. *He isn't speaking much. I think he should see someone.*

He hung up: looked up and down the room. There

was enough Żubrówka for him to pour one out for the radiation in his heart. But it felt like robbing the tabernacle. He looked from Ron to Jane, to the infomercial on TV. Who were these people?

He took out his phone and re-read The Number's texts like an invitation to the Last Supper. He stepped into the hall at the top of the stairs and Jane ran out to tug his pantleg. She was just like a cat. He did not want to look at The Number in the presence of Jane, but he kept looking.

"30K," he texted The Number.

Almost before he hit Send, it came back "50K."

He would have to sell his gold. "Meet me in Chorley Park in the next two hours."

He went back in the room and bent over Ron's hefty yellow face, the skin cracked like a clay road. He kissed the man's forehead. Ron seemed to move one eye under the display case of his being, but Rick wasn't sure.

"I'll be back in a few hours," he said to Ron and Jane, neither of whom seemed to understand. "Nod if you understand."

Ron flushed like a sky about to storm. The old man's pain, the staleness of this resting place, made Rick recall a funeral procession as a kid through cold Detroit shanty-towns to a graveyard, and he almost cried, remembering his great aunt. This world was not serious—why should he be rustled if some freaks extorted him, if Facebook banned him, if he had to throw some money at the Society for the Suppression of Vice, because he was done with it, with being a pervert on a sad ideological crusade, a cloned rat on someone's treadmill.

He had to do this last thing before he went away.

"Stay with your dad," he told Jane when she followed.

a. beaumais

He watched as she got under the covers with Ron and got out her iPad and, step by step, he tiptoed away from her once her eyes were glued to the screen, to some video of a house burning.

*

"$80,000."

Rick swallowed as the teller, a greasy strand of hair dangling over each temple, stared at him and his suitcase.

"I don't know if we can do that," the teller said, darting between his screen and Rick's face. "Did you call ahead? What do you do for a living?"

"I'm a forex trader. I'm self-employed."

"Wait," said the teller, intonating the way you'd address a drug dealer rather than a currency dealer. Rick could sense his bad physiognomy—sweaty palms, stupid-eyed slouch, phlegmy voice. He knew he deserved this treatment. He wasn't really a currency trader, or much of an entrepreneur, but this was the title he presented. He was no higher on the bell curve than a mid-tier drug dealer.

The teller returned to his booth with an office worker who had a Cantonese surname and an oily forehead.

"We can only do $62,000," said the teller.

"Is there a problem?" asked Rick.

"No. It's just… No, that's just what we have to offer." The other man left.

"What about U.S. funds?"

"You have a U.S. account?"

"Uh huh."

"Dwayne, c'mere."

dox

The other man came back and typed something in the terminal.

Dwayne said, "We can do 23,500 U.S."

"I just want 15. Make that 20."

Rick's phone rang. It was Bela.

"Hey!" he said.

"Why were you at my house?" she asked.

His brain splooged like he was chaturbating on Xanax. He stood tall, fighting reality with his bare hands. All his life's mistakes grew like a vine around his neck but he just needed one more chance. His heart flooded with thankfulness.

"I had to apologize to you. I had to see how your dad was doing."

"Sign here."

"Hmm."

Rick didn't know what to say. Bela's breathing was a thermal vent at the bottom of the ocean.

"Has your signature changed?"

"No."

"You were evil yesterday."

Rick raised his arm as though to grapple the ceiling. "I know! I know! It's a part of me I want to bury. I want to do better for you. I want to be a different person. I want to–"

He looked down and re-signed beside the x. He almost said *grow old with you*—maybe he should have.

"Where are you?" she asked.

"At the bank–"

"Excuse me, Mister, um, Speer? People are waiting in line. Can you help us get through this? You are being discourteous."

Rick turned around to see sheep with manila folders.

"Hold on, please," he said into the phone. He wanted

to tell the greasy teller that he didn't know why his job hadn't been automated, that he should read Michael Hudson on the FIRE economy, but he just listened to Bela's breathing on the phone and almost floated off the ground, wishing he could capture the sound in a white-noise machine beside his bed.

The teller said something and gave him two envelopes. Rick walked off and put them down on a table with pens attached to strings.

"Hi," he said.

"Are you coming back?"

"Yes. Soon. As soon as I can. Bela—"

"OK. Tell me when you're coming."

"I will." Her voice was like a flute ruffling his hair.

"Come now," she said.

"I need to go to the park in the next hour. To do business. Chorley Park."

"Maybe I can come by there."

"Yeah. Actually, don't. Don't. Really don't."

"Why?"

"I have to do something. Just, trust me. I can't wait to see you."

"What are you not telling me?"

"Something happened to me. I'll explain later. I want to see you."

"You're kind of scaring me."

"No." He came to in the worst way, his eardrums ringing.

"No?"

"Just wait. I—"

He hung up and immediately wanted to call back and apologize, reassure her, but he didn't, because he didn't want to explain what he was doing. He knew he had to tiptoe away from his whole path dependence, his semantics, the screens he looked at, knew he had to find a perch in the sky and nuke his brain chemistry. He wheeled his suitcase outside and sat on the curb to message TORONTO IRON FIST /22/ and The Number. His hands shook. He could not go in naked. *This is my last stand*, he thought feebly. He would change his name, dye his hair, leave Toronto.

He had nobody.

He Googled security guards. He filled out a broken JavaScript contact form for Top Event Experts and surfed onto Craigslist, onto no-picture ads for men with bad grammar and exotic certifications. He tried a number and got a voicemail. *The customer you have dialed has not initiated their voicemail.* He saw another name on the screen: *Calvin J. Rinkelhorst Security. Ontario Security Licence. CPR/First aid training level C. Fully trained black belt. Heavyweight. Celebrity experience. Firearms safety. USA-bred. Mercedes-Benz pickups. Bang for buck. Excellent! Very honest. Your not going to regret Rinkelhorst excellence. 6138728081.*

He called.

"…yella?" like a mafioso rolling over from a hangover.

"Hi, I'm looking into buying security services. Can you tell me your rates?"

"Hold on," Calvin said. "Gettin' coffee. What you lookin' at? Event security. Executive protection. Kay. What?"

Rick swallowed. "I need to perform a transaction, like a handoff. Actually, two. In a park."

"I dun' wark with drug syndicates. Ya know I get rewarded if I tell my friend down at the station about folks like yas, but I'll let yas off, just awoken."

"No, it isn't drugs."

"Then what?"

"It's just money," said Rick quickly. "I have to pay some money to some people. It has nothing to do with drugs, guns, anything illegal, nothing."

"Then *what*? Cut to the chase. Pal."

"It's about my reputation."

"Ooosh. I see. I'm sorry. That's rough. Didn't mean to kick you like that while you's was down. I know how it can be out there. Owe yas an apology."

Rick waited.

"So gon' be pruhsumpchus and say someone's got dirt on ya."

"Exactl–"

"Gotcha. How long you need? Educated guess."

"About an hour?"

"Gotcha. Describe the transacting party. Big, small, armed. How many."

"I'm not sure. Probably not big—I mean, not strong. I don't think they'd be armed with much. With that much."

A convertible Corvette with a rich guy and his kid pulled into the parking lot, its bumper almost kissing Rick's nose. He was not making his case well. He just wanted backup—knew it wouldn't solve anything—just wanted to pay for it the way an obsessive wants to wash their hands again.

"Don't seem like I could help you, son."

"What's your normal rate?"

"Well… Well, about 300 per hour." He sounded gap-toothed and breathless.

"I'll give you $1,000 for the hour."

"What day you lookin'?"

"Right now."

"No, no, no. My insurance wouldn't cover this when we can't sit down first and work out the particulars. Ya over ya head."

"Please. $2,000. U.S. I'll give you a security deposit. Just get in, get out. If it's unsafe we turn back."

"10K deposit. Where do we meet at?"

Rick told him the intersection of the bank.

"You need me to drive?"

"Yes."

"Really? That's another $45."

"Deal," he said. It was cheaper than the ANTIFA delivery fee.

"Last thing: who are ya? Give me a good reason I should help ya, and a reason I shouldn't."

"Because I need to tie up some loose ends before I disappear. I'm trying to make things better. And there is no reason you shouldn't help me."

*

Rick fidgeted on the curb, his winter-damaged phone battery dropping under 20%. He closed some apps and entered Battery Saving Mode. He had messaged the two parties and staggered the meetings at Chorley Park by 15 minutes. Hadn't eaten or pissed in hours and did not like being out in the elements like a squeegee kid, although maybe it was good for him, maybe he deserved it. Maybe this was the impetus, once he legally changed his name, to stop living from Amazon package to Sugar Baby, from takeout to clickbait. Maybe he'd work on a rice farm in Thailand.

He thought of going back for his car and hightailing

the fuck out of Toronto, maybe down to Chile or Argentina if that was possible. But he'd have to see Ramesh at the condo and pass through the U.S. border, and if his name was all over social media, they'd see it when they Googled him. They'd sit him on a plastic chair in a paint-stinking room at the Niagara Falls border and make him advocate for his cause, for the contents they'd find on his phone after instructing him to leave it in his car. *Yes, Officer, I understand what you're seeing on there. I understand that, sir. How do I put this... do you know what the Cathedral is? Sir, I'm not a Nazi. I know my surname sounds like an SS member. Do you use the Internet? It's weird, the people you find there. And I got sucked into this—these are systemic forces bigger than us. Sir, if you went on 4chan and MPC, you'd know what I'm saying—sometime in 2014, there was a leap backward in the human race, very hard to describe, a singularity, an auto-immune reaction to corporate humanity, where it was no longer safe to not have an opinion. Officer, this is the void I stepped into, almost like there was a market for it, I swear I'm not a monster, I can't even change a flat tire most days and can't aim a gun and no, I can't hack into anything, I'm not part of the cognitive elite.*

Rick stood up from the curb, the crown of his head buzzing. He wanted to shower at his condo. Paying the Danegeld wouldn't get him more than a few yards out of the woods. There was no hotline for Internet extremists to call.

His thoughts were a tongue sea-sawing over concrete.

Retire to a cabin like Ted K.

Be in the park in 45 minutes. He tried to quarantine neurotic self-talk. His limbs were failing. He went across the intersection to Tim Hortons and dragged his duct-taped luggage into a wheelchair bathroom. The toilet was refilling and a strange odor like cheese whiz marked the place as recently run through, a toilet-paper square squirming over the vent. Bathrooms should be burned down and rebuilt every few months. He booted the toilet lid down. He pulsed over it with his hamstrings, almost wrapping the lid with a shell of toilet paper.

He slid his phone out and the screen flared, boobytrapped with notifications. His phone was full of crimes, the babbling song of his penis. He was hungry. Sometimes he liked to starve himself. He tried to resist the phone but he started fingering through it with no more reserve than a baby clenching on a bottle. This stupid phone whispering the language of his dick. It was why he met Bela, why he hunched over his desk angling for greenbacks. Sweat ridged his spine like he'd swapped organs with a pterodactyl. He knew this state—this halo of thwartedness would appear seconds before his thumb started scrolling thots on the Internet. He didn't know what made him cycle through these pictures so fast. There was nothing he did faster—like he was surfing a tidal wave and raising his arms to the heavens, his escape helicopter rising out of the sea.

He opened his Gallery in the cloud and found a pic he'd taken outside the Airport Ramada two years ago. It was the only thing that could distract him from the pain.

Voices under the door ordering donuts.

That first girl he'd paid for. Big sultry lips, coconut shampoo, pink g-string. Fuck yeah, haven't seen this in a while. Not quite his ATF, but there was something holy about the first time. His gut in pretzels as he parked the car and snuck past the guys at the front desk—two guys like Ramesh—and got in the elevator. Slammed 29, the floor the SMS said, and soared into the sky, into a honeypot or paradise. The doors dinged open and he moved like a test subject towards room #2912. He knocked twice, not loud. Sarita opened the door, their eyes caught, she was even hotter than the pictures, and she dodged back towards the beds as though to escape him, as though she'd jumped into a freezing lake or a syringe had delivered a stupendous, slightly allergic dose in her bloodstream. The moment of purity and judgment, the crossing of an underground river lined with burning oil barrels.

His life was over.

When he left down the elevator, and passed the reception (who didn't even look up from the computers), and got back in his car, without getting his cheekbones mashed in by pimps or feds, without giving his real name, without spending more than a dinner for two at a cheap steakhouse, then he didn't know how he'd carried on before, how anyone could be so stupid around women.

More pics of Sarita? He needed to drag his body out of this stall. But: there were two: one bethonged and hyper-airbrushed from the back, her curly ebony locks wet and hairsprayed, another showing her chin and a hat covering her eyes, a low-pixel phone number pasted diagonally, although maybe she'd stolen this pic from someone. When he rated the girls on the punter411 BBS, he'd always write a paragraph on how they acted when they opened the door and acclimatized to the new gravitational situation. This was his signature observation, for which some of the johns and all the SPs called him creepy, but his reviews were the most upvoted on the site. His ATFs were young girls who, when they realized he was young, wanted to peer inside his traumas over rosé, girls who hadn't yet turned jaded and would no doubt disappear months later when their uncles or exes found their ads, girls who'd otherwise be wholesome except for some childhood diddling or high-school insecurity, who for one night only would suck him bareback as they giggled at him, asking gently what was wrong with him, where he'd gone wrong and why he wasn't a prince.

Was he extreme?

He typed on his phone, *Leave bathroom with suitcase, get on plane.* He scrolled the pictures, found Flame, his penultimate TOFTT MILF. Thirty-eight, tanned, puckered face that could be southeastern European or Colombian, fake blonde but nice, fake tits but nice. He'd read reviews on punter411 saying she was a clockwatching, timewasting ghoster with a pimp orbiter bf—but that she was best in class for mature. She bailed twice before he offered $500 for the h/h; she told him to get to Motel 6 in 20 minutes. He had no plan to enter the room, let alone give her 500, but he laughed and tweeted his way to the motel, as though under a spell, and took, as instructed, the fire escape up to the third floor. He made it into the room after hallway eyeballfucking by a guy in a leg cast, the entrance, the first few seconds, her liminal-zone expression, entirely uncategorizable. Flame was meanspirited, but once she saw that Rick didn't care if she insulted him, she smiled more and finally stopped nagging and reminding him again and again not to sit on the second of the twin beds, the one by the window. When he found her creaming over him in reverse cowgirl and got an HPV scare about the condom slipping, he hopped off to the bathroom to run hot water over his dick and apply a new rubber, hardening himself with the thought that she'd resisted full kissing, full DFK—there was something to hope for.

The sight of the unicorn MILF made him skip across

the carpet and spank his ass and fly onto the forbidden bed by the window, where he landed on something hard. Flame came screaming at him like a mother bear to a wolf and Rick jumped again on the bed, on the hardness, which roiled under the sheets like a sea monster, and he heard "sheeeeeeeiiiiiittttt" as a skinny sallow black man in a du-rag crawled out from under the bed, looked at Rick in a karate pose, looked at Flame, and ran out.

Two days later he bought an escort review board for $25,000, wanting to update it from the flashing malware-metastasizing vBulletin to something sleek and Tinder-ish—maybe an app. But he was advised against this—creating an efficient platform for an illegal service would attract the feds. (His biggest secret was that he'd made more money off the escort review board, through selling the SPs advertising and the right to delete negative reviews, and ultimately selling the site for bitcoin, than he'd ever made off day trading.)

Someone knocked on the bathroom door. He'd forgotten everything.

"One second," Rick yelled, but it came out "one servant."

He scrolled through to Rachel, his true ATF, the one who ruined him. (He ruined himself.) He spoke German to her. Knew she was from Europe, maybe Moldova, but she wouldn't say. She was in college and didn't kiss back. He fell in love with her the first time he came through the door and she looked at him so adorably, her dark reddish dyed hair billowing over her neotenous cheeks—so adorably frigid, with nothing in all the riches and wisdom of the ages that could move her. It put a multiplier effect on everything she did. She could make a one-egg omelette that jet-fueled him through the night, could put a dab of lube on her index finger and turn his shaft skyward when normies wasted the whole bottle on his flaccidness, she could make sweatpants and running shoes into some industrial airport hangar fetish gear.

More knocking, but this was his favourite part. Once, after he'd taken Rachel to the steakhouse and movies and she was bent creamily over his bed and he—he should stop, should surrender to Bela, give her his remains—he was drunk and ruminating on some analogy for his pleasure—that fucking Rachel, the sunset zenith of the sexual rollercoaster, was like eating at his favourite Jewish steakhouse, but he said it in German, stumbling on the verb. She slapped backwards and stopped bucking and turned her head, her perfect Ruthenian peach face speaking a perfect wavelength of standard High German back at him, German that ridiculed him and called him *täuschen* and said he had the gut of a starving villager and brought him the greatest humiliation—he couldn't even make out half of what those dark eyes were saying but enough to know he wasn't high-agency Bateman, which only made his dick stiffen harder than ever, and he flipped her on her back and tried to kiss her but she reached for his mouth and covered it and pushed him, turning the cheek. He started to cry, his dick engorged and breaking the sound barrier as tears splashed over her and she wiped them furiously and then finally let him kiss her and he pumped harder, pinning her down and sobbing as he slipped his member out and in one deft move shed the dome and stuck her again till the blood started collecting from his toes and his brain and migrating through his torso till he exploded with life-ending spunk and rattled and she felt it and punched him in the jaw as his heart stem detached and she tore up his condo looking for

Xanax and aspirin, which she shoved down his throat as the ambulance came.

Pounding against the door. Rick grabbed the handle of his suitcase and went out. A squat bleary kinky-haired woman with dirty striped tights charged through, Rick wanting to cut his dick off, his mind moored to the toilet.

He passed hordes lined up for donuts.

Maybe he could give Bela all his money and jump on the train tracks. Twenty-six was long enough to live.

*

"Where are you?" the message said.

Rick crossed the street to the bank, vacuoles of thoughts inflating like helium balloons.

A man in an SUV three spots down flashed his headlights; the auto-locks clicked. Rick could feel sensors in the man's eyes scouring him as he thought, not having washed himself in the Tim Hortons bathroom, "I look like a ███████"

He opened the passenger-side door and climbed onto the leather seat. Calvin was stout like a condiment bottle with a David Simon circle-head, a gelled window's peak and a blazer. He shook Rick's hand lightly, revealing two missing bottom teeth and a spritz of cologne as he said, "Great to meet you."

"Now how we gonna execute this. You got the deposit? And my payment? Any transaction items. Maybe you already got a checklist in ya head?"

"I've got all the cash." Rick remembered: "I haven't divided it out yet."

"Your first mistake," said Calvin. "Where's this

dox

Chorley Park?"

"I can direct you." Rick remembered: "Wait, my suitcase!"

"Hell."

Rick opened the passenger-side door and saw a bank clerk looking at his suitcase, almost prodding it, circling it from multiple angles like a golfer.

Rick wheeled it away and the clerk threw his hands up angrily. Rick tapped the SUV trunk and Calvin unlocked it and got out to make some room for the suitcase among splintered wooden crates. They got back in and Calvin glanced over.

"Ya ready now, miss?"

"Let's go." Rick took out the two envelopes and divvied up four piles on his leg and the dashboard—one for Calvin, one for each of the ANTIFAs, one for himself.

At a red, Calvin looked over and said, "Jeez, son, ya gonna bring heat upon both us."

Calvin kept muttering Baltimore or Detroit slang, some kind of sideways adaptation to industrial annihilation, but Rick was not listening. Calvin asked him about his bandaged hand, the mark on his neck, but he didn't have any words. He didn't feel stupid, exactly—if anything, he felt a bassline of contented hunger under the treble of the post-MDMA. He felt serene and about to collapse. He kept thinking of Bela smiling last night. He put the two ANTIFA ransoms in the envelopes.

He was glad when Calvin took a wrong turn because it gave him an opening to say something. "Wrong way," he said. He focused on the next half-hour of his life as bugs burrowed under the saran wrap of his low-serotonin state. Rick did not usually get nervous, because he had few day-to-day demands and knew, in a world without mammoth hunts and holy wars, that it was maladaptive. He gave Calvin $12,045 and Calvin pulled down a shelf and put it there, staggering this motion at the last second by rotating and thumbing through it with one hand. From the rear-view mirror a badge dangled with gold leaves sprouting from eagle wings, along with a Shriner's-type hat and Greek letters.

"We need to go over some protacahl," said Calvin, two minutes from the park.

"I'll stand beside you doin' the transaction. I have a taser in my breast pocket," he said, patting it. "Last resort. Do not under any circumstance, under any I mean it, escalate the situation if the other party stands tough. Who are these folks?"

"They're from ANTIFA—antifascists."

"'What does that haff to do with you?"

"They found out I work for some websites they don't like and they're trying to ruin my life. One of them has a YouTube video with my friend in it."

"I believe in freedom and small gubment," Calvin said, as though saying a password. "Can't even get a fuckin' gun in this country."

"You're American."

"Maryland. The county. Worked in south-side Chicago. Detroit. Ballll'damore. I been everywhere man."

Rick didn't say anything, but Calvin went on: "Was a regionally ranked lightweight till the knees gave out." He sounded whimsical as he coughed up a lung. Rick almost grabbed the wheel.

"S'okay, junior."

They pulled up outside the park. Rick didn't know what to make of Calvin's glassy eyes, the gulf between his and Calvin's chemical imbalances, different cocktails of ruin, different reasons for lying awake at night. The sky was mostly blue, the rest was mixed patches hanging low and dim, everything too Celtic to be unalloyed by a few thoughts of falling into a cold stony ditch to die. Rick perceived in himself an emptiness of spinning wheels, a bad mood that he would normally conciliate by raiding his nootropic stash and stacking with riboflavin, racetem, intellect tree.

They walked the path, Calvin limping with diagonal steps like a waltz box.

"Ever thrown a punch?" asked Calvin.

"Once, about five years ago. In a chocolate store."

"Dear god. Look at me." He assumed a pose, elbows down, chin tucked, and Rick quickly mirrored it, without thinking—the swing, straight wrists, planted hips.

As soon as he stopped, the memory of it floated into mist.

Calvin said, "You know what, forget about all that. Go for the balls. You can kick? Everyone can kick. Ya voice is your main artillery."

They both went for a bench. "Where we s'possed to meet 'em?"

"I didn't set a spot. What about here?"

"You kidding me? Half the neighbourhood would see ya passing envelopes. Jeez, I think I'm getting old for this, or you are too damn young."

Calvin chuckled like he'd completed a wordplay rubik's cube. Calvin's toothless face was like a fly ribbon attracting Rick's evil thoughts. But he needed to believe the wiseguy branding was underwritten by real policy.

A man with a poodle passed on the path and nodded at Calvin, as though Calvin was the dominant party, and Rick thought that maybe Calvin *did* know something—maybe he was a professional. He had to believe in something.

"Fucking guy tries to stab you, don't face 'em head-on. Use your forearms to block 'em."

"Got it."

"Let's *do* this, Mr. Speer! Anything smells bad about these people and I'm paging out to my buddy."

Rick wasn't sure if pagers still existed, if this was slang for texting. He suddenly felt regret about the whole thing, like he'd backed himself with military precision into the stupidest, most piss-stained corner of the universe. The blueness of the sky battled his flashing nervous system; the colour blue was causing him brain damage.

"You still ever box?" asked Rick desperately.

"I teach. Coached Micky Valera about four and a half, five years back. Yonkers kid, good kid. Woulda gone on to't least unseat fucking Jones if he had've had his head screwed on right." He paused, thinking: "Ya head screwed on right is *everything*. It's what kills me about these kids I see through the years down the ages, my friend. Fuckin' major depressive episode, Jesus."

Rick wanted to believe Calvin had faced off with extreme egos, roided out people from splintered families who'd go to war in their bare feet. Would he even take Daryl in a fight? Maybe he'd tase him. Daryl's forearms were so inflated by pianos they'd knock over any coach past his glory days.

"Let's, why don't we say, we go to that tree by the bridge. Message your boys."

The idea of them being his "boys" made him dry-heave. There were no fucking boys. He messaged TORONTO IRON FIST /22/, telling them he was waiting for them "by the bridge" and that they had 30 minutes to collect the cash. He wrote the same to The Number, except specifying an hour and saying to not come straight away.

"Do not issue orders," wrote The Number.

"What'd they say?" asked Calvin when he saw Rick's face.

"I can't really tell."

"What's that?"

TORONTO IRON FIST /22/: "OK."

"The one group said OK."

"And the other group?"

"Sorry," he wrote The Number.

They sat on a bench watching pigeons behead themselves in cellophane bags. Rick's heartbeat was coming online, was pulling up like a horse at a cliff's edge. He texted Bela, saying not to come, then texted her again, telling her really not to come—that it was dangerous, which he immediately regretted. He tried calling her, but it went to her full voicemail. He could almost see vespers rising over the trees, the chirping of the earth, a drawer of evil sliding open, black bloc donning their masks, tucking away plastic penises, taping down piercings, hiding broken bottles in sleeves.

"Do you think we're going to be OK?" Rick asked.

"You mad? You think I should call backup?"

"Yeah."

*

At 6:49 p.m., under the big pine tree with Calvin, Rick, his nerves running in apocalyptic flight patterns, skin stirring like a mummy resurrecting, saw the first signs of black bloc in the park. Three figures walked side by side down the path in baseball caps, sunglasses, workboots. They neared and Calvin perked up as Rick took in what looked to be bandanas tucked in, goggles dangling from one guy's chest. They walked as a unit, not in synch but as a kind of bug army, marshalled by a beating horde-heart. Rick wanted to go the other way.

"What do you think?" he said to Calvin.

"Don't think much."

A plain homey girl and a tights-under-shorts jock paused in the middle of their jog to stretch, and the black bloc paused. Rick wanted to yell something and even opened his mouth to say "hey" but Calvin put out his hand like *chill*, and after Rick stared into the trees for a minute and wished he could take Vyvanse and wander along the Beaches all night ████████████████████████████—the joggers ran off. The black bloc resumed their march, and Rick knew any delay could increase the chances of the two transactions intersecting. The three black bloc pulled up their scarves like MS-13.

"You didn't mention you had backup," said an ANTIFA, now wearing goggles.

Rick hesitated.

"Do you have the cash?" asked Goggles.

"Yes."

"Let's see it."

"Did you delete the video?" said Rick.

Goggles cursed and shook his head and said, "What does that have to do with anything?"

"Why else would I give you the money?"

"Because you're a Nazi piece of shit? Because we're taking your fucking money?" said one with a Rojava flag t-shirt.

They sniggered with high-pitched, irony-bro energy,

like they'd spent their suburban lives vaping and listening to anarchist podcasts in a basement.

"Leave if you have nothing to offer," said Calvin.

They looked at each other and Goggles said, "I'm kidding. You think we came for a circle jerk?"

"Delete the video and I'll leave the money right there on the rock," said Rick. "My word."

"Your word?" said Goggles.

"Give us the money first."

Calvin stepped forward: "Give you one-fifth. Then you delete it so we see it gone. Then we give the rest and you leave."

The third ANTIFA, indistinct except for his pallor, said "yeah." Goggles murmured "fuck no" and Rojava said "what…" and then "yeah… yeah, I guess."

No one moved. Rick calculated a fifth of $11,000 and took it from an envelope, counting it under their glare and double-checking it was from the right envelope. He looked up and down the path, through the trees, and, seeing movement in the distance, possibly someone sitting on a log with a dog leash, he put the cash on the rock, covering it with a short dirty stick.

Goggles stepped forward and snatched it up, counting it like a cage cashier, then recounting. "OK."

"Your move," said Rick.

"I'll message my partner."

Your scat fetish movie partner?

Calvin made a hurry-up motion with his hand.

"OK, should be good."

Rick took out his phone and loaded the TORONTO IRON FIST /22/ account on YouTube. "It's still there."

a. beaumais

Rojava smirked. "Well, I guess you should give us more money then, you crypto-faggot."

Rick was always surprised when rainbow militants sprinkled in un-PC slurs, as if they were given a quota. He felt faint. Calvin grabbed his arm.

The ANTIFA laughed at him and he said, "Maybe you can snort coke off each other's buttholes as you recite Bookchin and prepare for the revolution."

"Ooooh! Good idea."

Calvin put his hand up. "You either delete the video and take the money, or you leave the money you took and you leave. Y'all are acting exceeding unprofessional. My support is arriving in a few minutes. Hell's Angels. Not sure he would see eye to eye with everything you stand for."

"K old man," said Goggles, through his teeth, as though he only de facto opposed Calvin. Goggles scrolled through his phone, maybe, maybe not deleting something or messaging someone—probably not—he wasn't pressing on the screen.

"OK, it's gone."

Rick looked at his phone. "No, it's not."

He realized he hadn't hit refresh. But when he did it was still there—replaced in the most recent position by a video of protestors marching with an anti-pipeline banner in a natural park.

"Hold up," said Goggles, the "up" accented non-Anglo.

Rick and Calvin looked at each other—Calvin making a pushing motion that Rick couldn't understand—*push them, attack them, hurry?* Rick almost cared more about the three black bloc leaving in time than with the video getting deleted. Daryl'd screwed him, and even if there was a grainy video or some search results related to a fistfight with black bloc, it was not like you could blacklist a piano mover. At most, someone someday could accuse Daryl of being a Nazi, but the whole world would be so submerged by then in VR shark tanks, so swimming with paper Nazis, that no one would notice.

Rick knew The Number would arrive soon, and if that transaction fell through, he'd be rated shoot on sight.

"Even if I pay you this," said Rick, "you can just post it again."

"No, no, we can delete it here," said the pale ANTIFA—they were all pale.

"I have it on this phone," said Goggles.

"You were in the parking lot outside my condo?"

"Yes." He pulled down his goggles to flash his eyes.

Rick didn't see them long enough to make a connection.

"I thought you had to ask someone before to delete it?"

Sniggers. "That was about permission."

"You can *watch* us delete it."

"How do I know you don't have a backup? Or someone didn't save it?"

"Um. You won't?"

"How will I know it's only on your phone?"

"Why would I just happen to have it downloaded and timestamped at the exact right time it was taken?"

Rick said nothing. He didn't care anymore. "Why should I trust anything you say?"

"I don't know. Why should we trust anything you say, Nazi boy?"

Calvin looked at him again. Everyone was looking at him.

"OK, delete it. Hurry."

Goggles smiled, flashing snaggle teeth, his ticket to

class warfare. "Hold up," he said, fingering his phone.

Rick stepped closer to Calvin, as though entering a new phase of the plan.

He stepped back to his original position.

Goggles grinned at his phone.

"Just getting more permission," Goggles said, no longer caring.

Rick looked at his phone: three minutes till The Number would arrive.

"If you don't have it gone in the next minute—and you need to show me—then the money's off the table."

"I don't see any money on the table. Why in such a rush, Nazi boy? Gotta go 69 with Richard Spencer? Don't want anyone to see you?"

"OK, we're leaving."

"Relax. I have permission now. Heh. Come over here."

"Is it off YouTube?"

"Yeah, come over here."

Rick checked YouTube and didn't see it.

"Ready?" said Goggles.

Calvin motioned with his hands for Rick to step forward. Rick moved with Calvin in formation, drawing closer to the dust-swirled pines, a delimitation of eternity. The ANTIFA were growing larger in his vision, getting closer, no longer holographic avatars but breathing entities who sweated, shitted, maimed. He felt scared, felt terrified by their feral eye sockets, confused by the smells in the air, like an abandoned basement of soggy cardboard boxes occasionally doused with cologne.

"See this?" said Goggles, drawing eyes to his dirty fingernails.

Rick looked at the shattered, vinelike screen.

"I'm going to delete this from the memory. When I see the money on the rock."

Rick slowly walked back, in a southeasterly direction, to the rock, where he lay the stack under the stick, all the while watching the screen in the distance, Calvin moving slightly out of synch with him, like the end of a whip.

"It's all there."

"I'm going to delete it at the count of three. Three, two, one." He waited another few seconds and deleted it.

"Goodbye," said Rick, gesturing at Calvin to leave with him.

"Wait," said Goggles. "Let me count this."

"It's the rest of the 11,000."

"Don't go anywhere," Goggles warned.

Rick didn't want to stop, but Calvin held out his hand to stop. Just then three men on bicycles flew past and circled around, wearing tights, camelbacks, and sunglasses over condom-esque head coverings like French grand prix racers, one with curly hair. Rick wanted to get the fuck out—didn't know whether to pretend he didn't know the black bloc or act like they were his friends. He did not trust anyone. "Calvin," he said, "let's go."

"Excuse me," said a new voice. "Is any of you named Rick W. Speer."

Rick turned to see the cyclists de-biking like dungeon gimps.

"Uh."

Calvin stepped between Rick and the three cyclists as the black bloc started murmuring.

"I see you already have friends here!" said the first

cyclist, like some undergrad econ lecturer.

"Who are you?" asked Rick. He did not know why he said this.

"We're your friendly neighbourhood cyclists, keeping the streets clean of scum." The man looked at the black bloc, his unshaven mouth grinning under the head-sock. He looked at Rick: "I've been sent here as a representative of she who conversed with you by text message. I will not be answering any questions about this exchange, but I will offer some conditions."

"OK?"

"Do you have the payment?"

Rick nodded.

"I've been told to tell you the following: first, that this transaction was your prerogative; second, that this is a voluntary donation on your part; third, that you cannot expect any result from this donation; fourth, that you cannot expect this donation returned under any circumstance. Do you agree to these four conditions?"

Rick wanted to run and scream, wanted to throw up. "Yes."

"Say it, then," said the man, taking out his phone and walking closer to Rick, recording him. "I, Rick W. Speer, agree to these conditions."

Rick looked around at the black bloc throughout the trees. He didn't want to say his name, as if not saying it was his last defense.

"I, Rick Speer, agree to these conditions."

"Give me the money," commanded the cyclist.

Rick stepped forward with the second envelope. Another cyclist was pulsating, triceps quivering through spandex, like he was on the cusp of lunging from the bike. The man started counting it rapidly, looking up when someone approached from the opposite direction. Rick could not see who it was—a couple taking a stroll, teenagers smoking weed? The man finished counting and stuck the envelope in a fanny pack. He zipped up and smiled.

"I see it's becoming a party here," he said. "Sorry to jet, but I'm in a hurry. It was a slice."

Three more black bloc came down the path, bearded, work-booted up.

The cyclists mounted their bikes.

"Where are you from?" one asked the black bloc.

"Where are you from?" they asked.

"Elmo sends his love."

"Smash the fash motherfucker!"

One of the new black bloc pointed at Calvin and the other ones nodded. Rick started to look for an exit. Calvin reached into his coat pocket. A black bloc feint-hit him as another smashed him over the head with a beer bottle.

"Oh no. Gotta run!" said a cyclist, and they took off.

Rick was far enough ahead that he could escape down the hill into the brush, into the streets. Calvin was limping, spitting out blood under a yew tree. An antifascist did a farmer's blow on him. Calvin keeled over, his head convulsing in its throes. Rick OK-Googled "call an ambulance."

"Fucking Nazi!"

"The other one!"

"I'm in Chorley Park! My friend's been attacked!"

Rick turned on his Periscope livestream as he got to the edge of the hill. He could not leave Calvin. He pointed his camera at the black bloc coming toward him like giant ants.

a. beaumais

He could not leave Calvin. Could not leave Calvin. Could not leave Calvin. He screamed. *This ends here.* He was not going to run away, was not going to fold himself back into society, into finger-traps of lies and psyops.

"I'm in Chorley Park. These animals have attacked an innocent man I hired as a security guard."

Seeing his viewer count reach 63, he turned the camera on himself.

"These people came after me because I help run a blog. If they kill me, I want you to see them."

He pointed the camera at them and moved towards them. They were rotating crablike, reaching into their pockets. One of them, sticking his hand out to block the camera, started running away after tripping on a stump. Goggles shouted at him as Rick walked towards Calvin and five black bloc encircled them. He put his hand on Calvin's back, rubbing it. Calvin was on his knees, tongue dangling, not breathing much. Rick did not film his face. "The ambulance is coming," he said. He wasn't sure if Calvin nodded or puked. He pointed the camera at Goggles and started towards him.

"Look at you. You're immortal now. Does that make you happy?"

A rock whirred past his ear.

"This is the end! We're at the end."

He hoped they would back off, but when they got even closer, he laughed.

"Take your money. You already maimed an innocent man!"

"Shut the fuck up," said Rojava, getting close, trying to snatch Rick's phone.

"Don't come any closer," said Rick. "Is this about

money? You want more?"

"Shut the fuck up."

"You can be the British, I'm the Germans. We can pretend it's Christmas during the war. No, you're the Kurds. You're the most perfect revolutionaries. Don't you see you're attacking the dregs of a dead power structure? We're all being used. All these battles have been set in motion by forces way bigger than us. We just had the psychological profile to get caught up in it. Here," he said, reaching into his back pocket and throwing the rest of his money to the ground. "Take it. I'm done with all this. The Internet doesn't exist anymore."

A black bloc crouched down, raked up a few hundred dollars, and started to run.

"Leon, get back in formation!" yelled Goggles. "I know where your son sleeps!"

Rick was undead; the ambulance would arrive, the backup would arrive, the police. The sun was almost down.

"Run!" said Rick. "See your family. Do somethi–"

A fist smashed his gut. He keeled over and took a boot to the temple. He released his elbow and hit a ribcage and spun forward as Rojava wheezed. A blood hose shot from his nose. He aimed the camera at Rojava. The scab on his hand was open and blood spurted on his phone. He pointed the camera at himself. Paused. Pointed the camera at Goggles, rotating around—a rock hit his hand and he dropped the phone. An ANTIFA leapt forward and stamped it out in a flurry of sparks.

His mirror unto the world gone, the sky sudsy water. The black bloc encircled him and he could not tell them apart. His rods and cones took in encrypted anger wrapped in scarves. The forms contorted and kicked his shins and he pulled back his fist and punched one in the arm and there was a gasp and the forms struck him in the chest, sliding wraithlike through the air. He heard the forest sigh, heard the thirst for blood in the trees. The reapers circled, tightening the noose.

"Rest in piss."

A siren in the distance. Calvin lay on the fuzzy earth, a few feet away, gone or concussed. Rick's hands were painted red and he heard his mother's voice singing him to sleep as a boy. The caped forms moved through the night. A boot appeared and knocked up his calf and he spilled onto the pine needles, tasting blood iron, tasting spores. He heard his name from his mother's mouth as the heavy ductwork in his ear pumped its penultimate vibration. His heart clawed and his vision collapsed till he wanted to be put out of his misery and red tears flew down his nose and he wanted to cry but it hurt and he had nobody left to cry for him. He wanted a boot to make him worm meat.

He heard his name getting louder, and he wanted to be with his mother, hearing her calling him to come out of the overheated van where he was sleeping so they could go swimming at the pool. He was not sure why time went on, why, and he realized it was Bela's voice. He got to his feet and called out for her. He saw her through the dark forms coming over the bridge in a red skirt. He could make out every detail of her—her glowing skin and bangles, her hair dark like a casket, how she floated on the grass praying-mantis-like. He shouted her name again through the forms and she came towards him smiling and crying. He tried to go to her but an elbow collapsed him and he fell and twisted his neck as Goggles restrained her. She pointed in his direction yelling something

and broke out towards him, "Is he alive? Is he?" and Calvin
stirred as the wind blew the grass over the blood. Rick rolled
to his feet, surrounded by three forms, and Goggles wrapped
his arm around Bela to shut her mouth. She bit down on his
hand and he punched her in the eye and Calvin started rising
up. Rick kicked someone's knee and broke towards Bela and
rained his bleeding fist down on Goggles' jaw and just then a
bicycle lock under the last of the sun and the new moon came
swinging at his head and his light was spent.

Politics at the Dinner Table

"**P**ass the potato pancakes," said Ariel.

Bela reached over the *bigaos* to give the potato pancakes to Ariel and Shahzad, sitting opposite her and Rick. She looked from Ron, at the head of the table, to Jane, across from him, where their mother used to sit. It was the first family dinner since Uncle Andrzej's funeral, and Bela'd taken the *bigaos* out of the freezer and reheated some potato pancakes and mushroom ravioli soup. Through her father's chewing and Jane's tugging at her sleeve she felt the tiniest trickle of sunlight through the stained glass, the germination of something under the trash of her life.

a. beaumais

She thought of her mom in the kitchen as the men wolfed down her food—could hardly believe her dad had come out for a few hours.

Ron poured out more vodka and everyone held up their glasses to give cheers, even Jane with her plastic mug of Kool-Aid. Bela downed hers and as the vodka ripped through her she said, "Guess what? I'm going back to school!"

She didn't know where this had come from—it seemed like the most life-affirming spasm she could have—but she smiled hard to solicit its acceptance. Ron rose to his feet to refill the shot-glasses. Bela felt an urge to put the brakes on her high energy—not because she disliked it, but because when she said or did such things she felt dread for the future. She knew that a few hours later her sense of well-being would be up in flames—she didn't take lithium anymore.

"What are you gonna take?" asked Shahzad.

"Japanese again. I think."

She always figured she'd commit suicide one day.

"One of my friends lives in Japan," said Rick.

Bela smirked, imagining this friend, whose *kanji* script couldn't be as good as hers, having discovered during her most recent semester *how* to learn—to read the *Yomiuri Shimbun* newspaper with her pop-up dictionary plugin and transcribe *Sailor Moon* and Isao Takahata and Satoshi Kon every night before bed, rather than cram textbook dialogues about ordering tea at an airport.

"He has Japanese kids and everything."

Bela pictured this friend, who probably worked for Nintendo or Toshiba, dressing his godly hapa children in their uniforms each morning before they walked single file along a mountain-side temple to school.

"Doesn't school cost money?" said Ariel.

Everyone stared at Rick—this was his cue—and Bela didn't know if Ariel'd told them about SeekingArrangement. All the staring distressed her, and Bela tried to redirect it to her sister: "Ariel, speaking of money, maybe you could, I don't know, do you think you could help with the mortgage payments for a few months? Then I could buy the course."

Ariel twitched her nose like she'd whiffed an alcoholic buffet fart. Bela laughed. She regretted bringing the mortgage payments up but also wanted to jump on her sister and strangle her. She sighed and the intractability burned through her like a pleasant acid. She would either stay silent around Ariel and resent her, or snap at her and feel guilt.

Shahzad looked at Ariel like, "That's reasonable, isn't it?"

"I don't know," said Ariel.

"Nevermind."

Ariel batted her lashes as though trying out a hypnosis technique from the Internet.

"So what do you do?" Shahzad asked Rick.

"He works for Richard Spencer," Ariel barked out.

"Woah. That's crazy."

"Richard?" said Ron.

"Richard Spencer," said Rick. "I have no connection to that guy. Everything he touches turns to shit."

Bela didn't know anything about Spencer—the guy who looked like a fat Arcade Fire backup singer—besides that he was the Pepe guy who got punched for being a Nazi. She was pretty sure her cousin had told her on WhatsApp that Spencer was a good guy, or maybe a *Niemiecki* bastard. She usually asked her friend Christian what to think about these types of people, when he took her out for dinner.

"Ariel," said Bela. "I don't think he knows him."

Bela went to her laptop on the fireplace ledge. As a white flag she changed the music from EDM to some chick who looked like a robot in the music videos and made boring "sound experiments" that Ariel blogged about. Maybe she'd message Ariel later about their relationship (probably not), but for now she wanted to change the subject—possibly by saying that she'd seen a documentary about female genital mutilation in Sierra Leone and how it made some of the women happy, at which time Ariel would open her binder of knowledge on female genital mutilation and no one would get a chance to speak for a while.

Bela went to the kitchen, calling out whether anyone wanted coffee. She took a tally: two coffees, two herbal teas, a Kool-Aid, as she heard the glug-glug of vodka pouring. She put the old coffee in the microwave. Shahzad and Rick discussed something local-sounding, the Toronto Blue Jays, or maybe Trinity Bellwoods. She wanted to go to garage sales in Trinity tomorrow, see if she could find something for her Etsy store, see if the girl on College Street with the triangle hips was having another sale so she could ask her out, but she'd probably already moved.

When it seemed Ariel had simmered down, Bela brought out a few plates of the cream pie she'd bought at Starsky's. Rick helped clear the table; Jane took the salt and pepper mills back to the kitchen. Ron was shovelling his *bigaos* mountain, looking the way he had in Międzyzdroje decades ago when he ate lobster in a bib, snapping claws with bare hands, surgically slurping protein.

Bela gave Rick his cream pie and reheated coffee. She

wondered if she was getting her period.

Rick said, "So, the Pomeranian."

"Not now," Bela said, looking slowly towards her father. "How are you feeling?"

"*Zjem trochę więcej.*"

He poured himself another vodka and did the same for Rick and, as an afterthought, Shahzad. Bela poured one for herself and drank it before she could think twice—as though slicing through construction tape at a building that wasn't finished. "It's so nice out today," she said. "I can feel the summer in my hair." She wanted to outrun anything in her head before it caught up with her. She didn't usually say things like this, but she was tremoring, poised on the edge of sleep deprivation and the changing seasons.

Jane took the stem of a yellow rose she'd bought at Metro and stirred the water in the vase. She followed Bela to the kitchen to help bring the rest of the cream pie to the table, but got distracted by a ladybug under the stairs, and Bela took her by the hand.

"I love how all the men are sitting around as the women work," said Ariel.

There was nothing left to do when Shahzad jumped up, and he laughed.

"I don't mind," said Bela. "I'm used to people only being here at Christmas."

Jane took Rick's hand and started reading his palm like they did in the YouTube videos she watched.

Bela poured herself a bump of vodka.

Ariel looked at Rick and said: "So, serious question."

"Shoot."

"How can you demonstrate that you're an ally?"

"Come on," said Shahzad.

"I'm serious."

Rick said, "I'll assassinate your neighbour. I'll poison him in his sleep."

Ron grimaced and then smiled, maybe understanding.

"How would you do that?" said Ariel.

"I don't know. How can you tell when he's home or not?"

"When his Oldsmobile in driveway," said Ron.

"Are you people fuckin' serious about this?" said Shahzad.

"No," said Bela. "Just no." She imagined a bathtub full of gasoline, lined with candles.

"Well, not the poisoning part," said Rick.

"OK," said Ariel, "that's, ahem, what you can do for my dad. What will you do for Bela? Pay her tuition?"

Ariel smiled like she was engaging in the art of the deal rather than shitting on dinner. Everyone stared at Bela. She felt like her skin was breaking out in hives. Sometimes she hated being looked at.

"I guess that would make me a real, as they say, card-carrying ally."

Ariel added, "And Shahzad?"

"I'll buy him a beer this week," said Rick.

"Not good enough," Ariel said. "And I'm not even joking. You have to perform some actual labour if you want to make inroads in this community."

"It's good enough for me," said Shahzad. "Maybe y'all can smoke a lil' of that icky sticky too?"

Rick had told Bela he hated people who smoked weed, that legalization was a plot to "groom" people for complacency. She got up to crank the music, which'd stopped, maybe due to insulation in the walls zapping the wi-fi. She stood there, hesitating. She needed ibuprofen for the cramps.

Ariel hissed. "And me?"

Rick grinned like a bear whose foot was caught in a small, ridiculous trap.

"I don't know."

"For a start, you can come to my talk tonight."

"But we have our concert," Bela said.

"What time does FJR come on at?"

"Nine?"

"So you'll come for half an hour."

"Ariel, no. Just stop. Seriously." They'd only gotten in one fight since Ariel moved out—when Bela left rings on Ariel's wrists that lasted a week. She looked over at her father, his face a burnt-out bulb. She knew the signs—he reverted to this mode until the void became a black halo and he started wheezing. Bela had to intervene. The men were hoovering their cream pie, a quiet punctured by the sound of Jane wringing cream through her fingers. Bela didn't know what to say.

"So," said Ariel, her voice wavering like she was introducing herself. "Here's the thing, my dude. What makes you think I'm going to accept someone like you in this house?"

Bela's pinched neck birthed a throbbing in her left quadrant. She tucked back her chin as she considered whether to lead her dad by the hand to his bedroom or punch her sister in the face.

Rick smiled: "Didn't I say I'd prove my worth to you all?"

"I'm serious," said Ariel. "We're not living in a world where cowboy patriarchal fascist bullshit goes unchallenged."

"Air," said Shahzad.

"It's OK," said Rick. "I have no idea how you get from libertarianism to fascism."

"Libertarianism is a limbo for Nazis before they reach their final circle of hell."

Ron told Ariel to shut up in Polish. It pleased Bela even though she wanted him to speak English out of politeness, but she didn't want to make him more red.

"Libertarianism isn't about group identity," he said. "Although it can be odious, sure—like, tax cuts for billionaires. Randian corporatocracy. But that's not real libertarianism."

"You'd rather just have white nationalism."

Rick looked at Shahzad, a bead of sweat catching the chandelier light. "I don't know how you get from A to B. I mean, sure, many of the people attracted to libertarianism might be white. But it's not about race."

"How is it not a bowtie for white supremacy, seeing as how you think it's superior and people of colour won't go for it?"

Rick swallowed like he had a sore throat. "It's about property rights. If you asked the governments of Beijing or Johannesburg what they strive for, it wouldn't be libertarianism, and that's fine. Is that my fault?" Very diplomatically, he added, "But I just met you. Why don't we talk about this later."

"Nuh-uh-uh. Let's just establish a few ground rules," said Ariel. "First of all, you should know that I'm not dense, so let's just establish that right away. Second, you're going to date my sister, or you think you are. You think I don't know the type of content your site publishes? You think you're going to hang around this house eating our food and then you're going to go home and pump more bile into the Internet? You think people aren't affected by what you do? My dude, you're a problem. I'm telling you this clearly. And if I don't call people out about this kind of shit, I don't see anybody who's picking up the slack. I see the people you associate with. We can't put this in a little box and file it away for a rainy day. We don't have that privilege."

Ron's face was all grey sweat, his ear twitching like a mackerel. He told her in Polish to stop and she said, "Shut up, dad!" and he slammed the table with his fist and left.

Shahzad blurted "woah" like he was about to do something.

"This is my family. This is my community," said Ariel, like it was a prayer.

"You're never even here," said Bela. "Why do you have to ruin this? Why do you have to make dad mad? He's not fucking *healthy*!"

Ariel raised her hand to make a speech. "Well, I'm here now." A tear was changing the shape of her eye like a contact lens. "I'm not interested in your type of civility. Or your boyfriends."

"Can you not do me this favour?"

No one spoke. Sunlight illuminated the stench of death.

"Fucking white men."

Before Ariel could speak again, Rick said, "I don't get it." He waited a second to look at Bela, then Ariel.

Ariel: "Get what?"

"White man bad. Blah blah blah. If white people are losing power, shouldn't that make you happy? Why would you expect any group to decline without a whimper?"

"You can't expect populations to stay the same," said Ariel. "And you can't apply historical norms to today, when we're this interconnected, when we're doing the work of undoing centuries of oppression."

"But no population ever gave up its majority status like this. Isn't that something the left should celebrate? If you guys had more patience, we wouldn't have gotten Trump."

"And the fact that it's voluntary means it's so bad, doesn't it? Doesn't that get under your skin the most, that most people in this city hate you?"

"I don't know if it's voluntary. The media and education system indoctrinate people, and anyone who disagrees is at best a nutcase but more likely loses their job."

"And immigrants are just so *odious*," said Shahzad.

"I'm just speaking in abstractions. I'm saying if you went to Korea or Nigeria and you started fucking with the demographics of those countries, they'd pause whatever conflicts they had and drive out the people fucking with them."

Shahzad: "So you want, what, some dictator to freeze things in place?"

Rick turned to Shahzad, surprised he had to argue on two fronts now. Bela wondered what Christian would say. She knew he wouldn't take Ariel's bait—wouldn't jump in the ring as her father pounded his fist.

"Libertarians want self-sustaining communities based on private property, private law societies, private policy. I guess it's a little autistic to—"

"Shut your fucking trap!" said Ariel. "You realize some people *are* autistic," she looked at Jane, "and it's not just an edgy word for Internet avatars."

"I'm sorry," he said. "I didn't know... she was."

"Agata," said Bela, "don't act like you're the one who deals with this every day."

Ariel bit her bottom lip as smug woundedness washed over her.

"The West is in a holding pattern of decadence and relativism," said Rick. "It's just historicism. And it creates a vacuum where people yearn for strength in ways that can be ugly."

"You need to get over it," said Ariel. "People of colour had their communities razed to the ground by our ancestors. For hundreds of years. I'm sure many of them would trade that for your naval-gazing bullshit. I'm so, so very sorry that white men have these issues, I'm sure it's a global crisis."

"I thought you guys were Polish? Poland never did shit to anyone."

Ariel said nothing.

He continued, "I wouldn't deny life is better vis-à-vis technology, medicine, convenience. But we've drifted away from healthy families, from virtue, from *noblesse oblige*, from any baseline level of consensus" (Ariel was laughing). "This kind of consensus, even if it's cruel, even if it elides over certain forms of injustice, is the foundation of civilization. It's why–"

"Fuck a baseline of normality. White cis men don't need to be accommodated any more than they are. You alt-right freaks cry about the decline of fucking morals, but you don't practice any kind of Christian virtue, because if you did, you wouldn't be such racist pieces of shit."

Rick scratched his nose performatively. "You appeal to Christian universalism to push your view, while also dismissing 'fucking morals.'"

"You don't understand your fucking religion," said Ariel.

"I don't have religion."

a. beaumais

"I thought you went to church?" said Bela.

Rick'd told her he went sometimes—that he'd started going again. She wondered if he believed in the Trinity. She mostly liked the way the thurible smelled when the priest swung it at Easter, liked dressing up with Jane on the 24th to celebrate Christmas with her father, to see him shovel *borscht* and *uszka* into his mouth.

"Agata," Ron called from upstairs.

"Romek, we're having a conversation. Someone has to tell this dude what's wrong with him."

Rick looked around to weigh his options, but Ariel waved her hand dismissively at her father.

Rick said, "Churches don't care who fills their pews. Businesses don't care who buys their products. Governments don't care who votes for them. I don't take it personally."

"So businesses shouldn't sell products to whoever they want? What kind of libertarian are you?"

"No, they should. But they need to be aware of the bad neighbour problem."

"Did you just graduate high school?"

The fridge radiated in the kitchen as Bela took her last bite of cream pie. She remembered playing in the yard at recess in grade four, eating Tupperware cream pie by the sewer drain behind the baseball diamond. A Polish boy named Przemek would fish cellophane out of the drain with a hooked string. She wondered if this moment had any continuity with those days—if she was actually the same person.

"And, just to put my libertarian bowtie on for a second, this isn't just a question of my psychic anguish or comfort. In every institution, we're seeing quotas and speech codes. We're seeing the end of free–"

"Why are you guys still talking about this?" asked Bela.

"People who clamor the loudest for free speech are the ones who'd take it away from others if they got in power."

"I'm a libertarian, not a fascist–"

Bela pushed her chair out. "Why don't you guys get a room if you want to talk like this. Seriously, I don't give a fuck about any of it."

Ariel waited a second before continuing: "Libertarianism is the exoskeleton of a fascist ideology. Libertarians don't oppose violence—they would just prefer the violence isn't in a remote desert but's about shaming single mothers in their own communities. And don't even try to pretend that people like Richard Spencer didn't come out of libertarianism."

"Richard Spencer–"

"Answer me this. What have you, as a fucking white guy, done about Richard Spencer?"

Rick swallowed three times in a row and Bela wondered if he was going to choke.

"Richard Spencer turns everything to shit. He's the shit Midas. The second he lays eyes on someone, they have to disavow. And he thinks this is this cosmic injustice. Like a problem child who doesn't realize he's being ridiculed, who can't stop shouting back. Why does he matter? His only plan was to go to colleges and give speeches about reconstituting the Roman Empire to five students."

"You're not answering the question."

"What do you want me to say? He's some dude who likes to travel to college towns and drink with his buddies. He says, 'homosexuality is the implicit last stand of white identity.'"

"Ew," said Bela, imagining fat alt-right men in turtle

helmets and tighty-whiteys sodomizing each other with batons. She could smell it.

"Richard Spencer disguises fascism with progressivism. So tell me, what have you done about Richard Spencer?"

"Nothing. He's just a twink LARPing like he's going to start a Patrick Bateman revolution where all the frat boys put on Ray-Bans and these unicorn WASP financiers come out of the woodwork and learn to laugh at the poor again and attend Wagner operas. And the race war starts as Spencer's shuttled like a Caesar between college campuses and basements, where he does podcasts with teenagers until the day someone comes on the scene who's richer, blonder, more Norman, and Spencer starts attacking him, because this threatens his beautiful self-alienation performance art, and he's too jealous, he couldn't even tolerate Milo or Bannon."

Shahzad smiled. Bela didn't understand Bateman or Norman or Milo. She took Jane by the hand to the kitchen, imagining them turning invisible, cloaked, flickering over the sink on a moon of Saturn, a Japanese colony where she could find love without earthly concerns. She scrubbed the *bigaos* crust with steel wool, her sense of control slipping.

Ariel said, "Are you talking about yourself? Looks like he's not the only Nazi who's jealous."

"Huh?"

"You should see the look on your face when you talk about him. It's good that the far-right hates each other so much."

"Who says I'm part of it?"

"What's the point of all this?" asked Shahzad. "What's your struggle if you're not part of it?"

Bela handed Jane a tupperware box to put away.

She turned on the tap, reminding herself to relax, that she'd only recently come out of hibernation—a deep physiological event precipitated by getting her heart staked to the wall. When James dumped her for Karla, she'd still see him every day outside textiles class because he TA'ed a course next door. She would stare at Karla and be blinded by the sun. The first time she met Karla was in the after-hours club when Bela was still dating James. Karla'd said something sarcastic to her and they'd all gone to the coat room to smoke a joint. Whereas the weed gave Bela a sad lip-licking warm bath feeling, it pricked Karla's eyes with something mystical and everyone stared as though a spotlight shone on her. Through the crossfire of conversations Karla said something to Bela, one on one, that Bela couldn't understand, and she asked her to repeat, and Karla repeated it, or said something new—Bela wasn't sure and couldn't look away because Karla hypnotized her like a black angel, had her nodding like a puppet.

Rick said, "I don't know. We can either have a society based on technology and order, one based on individualism and markets, or one based on human controllers who try their damndest to keep a lid on everything and pull the strings, which is what we have now. We're slouching towards the Cathedral— it's all morals, no mathematics. So what I'd want is for the world to take a hard step forward towards order and intelligence, while trying as hard as possible to preserve individual rights. We need a new consensus. We need fragmentation."

Bela heard Ariel spray something like orange juice on her plate.

Someone shuffled in their chair. "Hell, maybe the point of anything might be what we're doing now. Just enjoying the time we have. Learning to live with each other."

a. beaumais

Bela looked out the window at a squirrel vaulting branches, unsure if Rick believed this. Purple tinged the sky. Karla was probably the best-looking person who'd walked the earth, based on that single unspooling of seconds. She looked like a fairy, rail thin with auburn hair and a salting of cheetah freckles, a body that despite its thinness had hips and ass that were pale bulging mountains in a way that made people horny despite it almost seeming unsightly.

"It sounds like you don't want to be among humans," said Ariel. "Maybe you could move to a cabin in the woods and go crazy there. Because here, you're in the way."

Ron stood in the door: "*Agata! Zamknij się! Przestań!*"

"Don't tell me to shut up," said Ariel, rising.

Ron was panting.

"Ariel, fucking stop," Bela said.

"You're addicted to lost causes," said Ariel. "You'll never win. Your movement has no talent. You have a few bloggers and a bunch of anonymous trolls. Everyone you ever had in the White House was incompetent. Bannon's a disgusting pervert who took the wrong meaning from *Don Quixote*. And it makes sense—if you guys can't form a counterculture, how would you run a society?"

After James traded Bela for Karla, Bela invited him to a fashion show rehearsal with her classmates—more like a night to get drunk at a run-down theatre with a catwalk. She missed the old days at the after-hours club—hadn't had time alone with James in months. A Galician girl tried to invite Karla to the fashion show at the last minute and Bela reacted badly, texted the girl that Karla was a stupid bitch.

James came but it was no use—he'd moved on. She cried all night after the show.

dox

On the Monday, Karla was waiting for her outside textiles class in a tank top showing off her rose-thorn half-sleeves. She stuck her finger an inch from Bela's eye: "You're a stupid fat bitch and he doesn't wanna be with you! I saw everything you said about me. You think you can call me shit because I'm infringing on your special time with Jay?"

Karla kept yelling and threatening Bela in front of everyone, ignoring her apologies. "You don't understand. I don't give a fuck if you're a sad, jealous, mildly retarded bitch! It's not my problem."

Bela saw James leaning against the brick wall and said, "Are you hearing the things she's calling me?"

He shrugged stoically, said, "She's harsh, but I think she makes more sense than you."

Bela stopped going to class. She never wanted to see James (or "Jay," as Karla called him) again, but even more so didn't want to see Karla. She stopped going to Kensington Market and Ossington and anywhere Karla could find her. She turned into a k-whore and cut herself. She saved and catalogued all the Facebook and Flickr pictures of Karla, putting them side by side with her own to rate them according to a growing list of criteria, face, skin, eyes, breasts, ass, legs, smile, teeth (Karla had rat teeth), fashion. She went on anti-depressants, shaved her head, and dropped out of school.

"That might be tr—"

"We're going to win. We have the talent."

"No, billionaires are going to win."

"Well, we'll be second place then. And you can move to the woods because we don't need you, we don't need some racist Schopenhauer…"

"Schopenhauer was not ra—"

a. beaumais

Bela rinsed the last dish and went back to the dining room. Years had passed. She'd seen Karla once at a waterpark and secretly watched her splash around in the wave pool like a Suicide Girl. She'd look Karla up on Facebook every half a year, see whatever kitschy new watercolour Karla was selling to thirsty, unattractive men. But a few weeks ago, when she Googled Karla's name out of boredom, she'd found her obituary.

Suddenly, in Cancun, Mexico, in her 26th year, Karla O'Hara-Grimsby left this peaceful earth.

Bela binged on all the obituaries, funeral home guestbooks, Facebook comments. Karla'd gone to Cancun on spring break and died at a resort, but Karla's hippie parents had, it seemed, called for silence because every vaguely mutual friend of a friend who Bela prodded would say the same thing, that they were unsure of the details beyond it happening "outside." But Bela had to know: had Karla OD'ed? Had she died during a sex party? Food poisoning? It didn't make her happy, it made her heart palpate. But it scared her so much that she stopped staying up all night drinking wine in front of the TV and this gradually unlocked a thousand-pound steel cage from her face. She started working more shifts. She could walk around in the old neighbourhoods without facing her inferiority. It was like she'd been declared the winner of a contest she'd been disqualified from years ago.

Ron threw a plate at the wall and it smashed a portrait of the sisters' *babcia*. He went back upstairs as Ariel got up, sat back down. She was ghost-faced, too upset to yell, shuddering and crying out snot missiles. She looked both ways and walked out the front door, Shahzad following, and there was only Rick left and Jane, watching a video on her iPad. The front door slammed.

"Holy shit," said Rick.

Bela didn't know what to think other than that Ariel and Rick should either marry or kill each other. She picked up the shards of china and threw them in the trash—took them out in case they could be glued back, almost cordoning off the tiny jagged pieces on the floor before she could vacuum, but Jane was sucked into her iPad, out of danger, so Bela went up to the top floor, where Ron was watching the news at a volume too low to be real and finishing the dregs of a bottle.

Bela apologized.

She climbed onto the bed beside him.

She rubbed the back of his neck. "Is he bad, daddy? I'm sorry."

"What?"

"Is he bad."

"*Nie, jest w porządku.*"

She targeted the back of his neck, his pinched nerves, the way some people at clubs did for her. She felt the revving of distance between them as though they were on opposite sides of a rainy highway, a genetic distance unbridged by the simple fact of a shared connection to her mom—but she only loved him more for this.

He asked for ambien.

"Are you sure?"

"*Tak!*"

She went to the cubbie bathroom—a toilet and shelf hanging by a nail—the sink was in the bedroom—and took one from the bottle. Bela's friend had had to find him these from the dark web—his GP had cut him off after he started getting the shits and seeing visions of Father Romek from Lvov. She gave Ron a half and went back downstairs—stopped on a step and looked through the Saint Hildegard stained glass. Every glimmer in her life only illuminated how fucked up everyone was.

Rick was sitting at the table with Jane, scrolling through hundreds of CPR videos on her playlist. Bela thought, *Maybe he is ok.*

She said, "I'm sorry about tonight."

Rick shrugged. "This isn't my first rodeo."

"That's the first time she was here in three weeks," said Bela. She wanted to go on, but she felt it made no difference.

"Hey," she said. "Can you drive me to the store?" Ariel had stopped driving her at the start of the new semester.

"Sure. I guess I need to keep proving myself to you guys, right?"

Bela looked at Jane, who was extending her queue of YouTube videos infinitely. She wondered whether to send Jane upstairs to lie with Ron, or get her out of the house. "Do you want to come with us?"

When Jane was ready at the door in her pink Reeboks, Bela took the iPad from her hands and left it on the mail table.

*

Bela insisted on paying for the lemon juice, licorice, homo milk, spinach, Polish pickles, eggplant, Drumsticks, shredded coconut, Ricola, chia bread, Kotex, 6-pac of Tyskie for Ron, and discounted chocolate bunny, despite Rick waving his VISA over the point of sale.

They loaded the trunk of his Beemer and Jane refused to not hold the Drumsticks in her lap. They buckled up and Bela saw her sister staring glassy-eyed at Silver Rail Toy Shoppe, a family business that'd somehow held on beside the big-box stores and condos. Jane had woken up Bela last week at 5 a.m. to ask if they could visit the shoppe, as was their custom whenever Jane had a birthday or a "half birthday," which was next week.

"Do you want to go in?" asked Bela.

"Ya."

Bela got Jane to leave the Drumsticks and the three of them went in. Shelly, the aproned, Mia Wallace-looking daughter of the owner, asked about Ron as they examined a 1930s model train and marble works, a Grimm Brothers colouring book, a harmonica. Bela followed Jane to the costume section as Jane grabbed a Venetian mask with a scaly green fish-tail and black swirls.

"This one's cute," said Bela, picking up an orange jester mask with bells.

She held it out to Jane—it was half the price—but Jane was lost in the green scales.

Bela put on the jester mask and handed a bee-coloured half-mask with a Pinocchio nose to Rick. They stared at themselves in the mirror, at their shared phenotype of pale skin and black hair. She wondered if he was thinking the same thing.

Jane cried when they left the aisle.

"You can get the mermaid one," said Rick. Everything Shelly asked Jane at the counter—about her elephant slippers, about the tooth fairy, about Ron—went out the other ear. When Bela said Ron was "not the best," she felt her abdomen grind and she cried out. Shelly didn't inquire further. Rick took two *Scream* masks and tossed them on the counter: $182 all in.

a. beaumais

In the parking lot Bela told Jane to thank Rick and she hugged his legs, her arms snaking up around his torso.

"Now if only your other sister would love me like that," he said as they got in the car.

At a red light, Bela looked over at Rick reading Twitter. "Is that my sister?" Ariel's profile photo showed her wearing a name tag with some activists at a conference table. Rick swiped his finger rapidly as though the screen were a clit. He read off, "The queering of parenthood, how white cis women can overcome their privilege and become allies... how to write about undocumented children... Assassins Creed and BDSM... the time I met my childhood friend on FetLife... What's her description? She/her. Why do they always need pronoun tags? It's not like I'm going to speak to them in the third-person..." He let out a breath. "Whew. Where do I start?"

"You don't," said Bela. She looked back at Jane, dancing in her seat with her mask and Drumsticks.

"How does her boyfriend put up with it? Does he just dissociate?"

"I don't know. I don't really know him. I mean he's nice when we see him. But I only see him with Ariel. And he doesn't speak Polish or have anything in common with my dad."

"I don't think I could handle her talk tonight. It would be like a Tutsi going to a Hutu convention. And we don't really have much time. I'll have to make it up to her some other way."

*

On the drive home, Bela caught Rick looking at her.

"What is it?"

"I just want to look at you."

*

Bela set the grocery bags down on the granite counter. She thought Rick was leaning in to kiss her, but instead he said, "Do you want me to talk to your neighbour?"

"We already did."

"But it didn't go anywhere."

"No."

"Let me try. I know how to get through to people."

"What are you going to say?"

"I'll ask if I can see his property survey. See if we can get this resolved, see what it takes. If there's someone who actually needs a favour, it's your dad."

Bela no more wanted to go next door than she wanted to talk to a telemarketer on her lunchbreak. She needed to sit on the couch for five minutes. She was beyond damage.

"Please, no. Maybe tomorrow."

He held her by the hips: "Just trying to be useful."

Jane sat on a stool, her masked eyes tracking a lifeguard patrolling a pool in a video, saying, "No glass, no gas, no fire, no wires."

Rick said, "Let's drop by there before we go to the Portlands."

Fuck no. She had no strength left. She almost asked him to leave.

"OK?"

She stared at the ground.

"Just come on." He took her by the hand and she couldn't do anything—she felt like a DJ unable to put the cartridge to the vinyl, her hand limp. She would stand at the bottom of the steps if he talked to the Pomeranian. "Let's go," he said and she was taken by the hand out the door and across the grass, but she pulled him to the sidewalk and up the path beside the tree with the door in it. They climbed the paint-chipped wooden porch and she hung back as he knocked. The lights were off inside.

"Do you think he's home? Does he drive?"

Bela didn't see his Oldsmobile. She'd never made the connection before—his car was always there—but she felt that he was probably gone.

"I don't think he's home."

He knocked harder.

"Where are you going?" she asked, following.

He tried the gate to the backyard and she grabbed his collar. "What the fuck?"

"You said he's not there! So let's check if he's back here." He called out: "Hello?"

"You don't know what this guy is like. He doesn't act like a normal person."

"I've slain bigger dragons."

"You don't have to live here."

Rick opened the gate. A cherub fountain on the yellow grass. Under a maroon awning Rick knocked on the backdoor. Bela felt a rustle of evil like the grass contained bodies. She'd never been back here—the flowerbeds were empty except sallow palm stalks over dirt. A ride-on lawnmower frame rested on planks. Past the fence and pines, she could see her roof.

Rick knocked on the glass of the sliding door.

He tried the door.

"What the hell are you doing?" said Bela. "I'm leaving."

He stepped away from the door and tried the kitchen window. It slid open at chest level.

He peeked in.

"I said I'm leaving."

"Just wait. Two minutes. What are the odds he comes back? I feel like we're going to find something."

Bela took back every bad thought she'd ever had about her older sister. Rick was just another psycho from the Internet. She made for the gate and he called her name. As she opened the gate a red sedan started turning into a driveway across the street. She darted back, not knowing what to do, and closed the gate, ducking.

Rick called her name louder.

"Shut up!"

The cedar fence to her house was seven feet tall. She crawled over and looked through the Pomeranian's kitchen window as Rick held his hand over the grey counter. She kicked off her wedges and pulled herself through the window as if entering a cave, half-expecting a dragon to fly through. She knew her judgment was blunted by the acid she'd done recently. She would run away if anything happened.

Sweet mildew smell. Waffle maker, slow cooker. Beige Mesolithic fridge.

Bela felt a pulsating bolt of insanity, of mismatched debits and credits. She hallucinated freedom like it was a boardgame. She ran through the kitchen hall and tiptoed to the living room in the front, where a telescope was aimed through the blinds, right-facing—in the direction of the

Ogóreks. Knitted pictures of rivers and windmills hung on the cracked plaster. A parched scroll with a poem called "Until the End of the Roses." Bela felt like there would be a crypt to the Pomeranian's wife. She'd probably knitted the portraits.

"I feel like if there's something in the house, it's gonna be downstairs."

"I was thinking the same."

In the dim yellow she emailed Jane, who responded to all messages within two to three seconds—told her to watch for the Pomeranian's car, to message ASAP if he pulled in.

In the kitchen they opened a door to the broom closet containing a ridged Electrolux vacuum with a rope-like hose—closed it. Rick found the door to downstairs. "Thirty seconds," she said to him, as she saw an email from Jane: "ya ok."

They pulled a hanging string and a light went on. A mustard-eyed cat ran through Rick's legs. He tried to grab it, but it was gone.

"We need to leave," said Bela.

"Just 10 seconds. Let's go down."

Bela didn't see a message from Jane.

They crept down the stairs into a new sensorium combining the stale upstairs with something spicier, heartier, like beef jerky. Through the graininess Bela could make out an appliance, maybe an oven, in front of dozens of jars lining the wall. Brains or pickles soaked in the jars and blood-red light spilled under a door.

Rick turned on his phone light.

"We need to go," said Bela.

"Wait," he said, casting the light around—from the oven to the jars, to cables and signal splitters in the corner—

to a door. He opened it and more red poured out. Bela started counting down from 10. They passed through the door into a room with two conference tables and mounted metal shelves. Rick picked up something on a table.

Bela came closer and saw a stack of photographs, all depicting a radiator. Another stack showed the tree with the door on the Pomeranian's front lawn. A single photo of her house at nighttime. Her heart sobbed. Rick turned off his flashlight and they walked along pictures of tree stumps, a squirrel in a trap, a closet with a mesh of coat hangers. At one end of the room was a broken three-legged chair with a cord dangling from the top. Bela felt dizzy and wanted to diffuse essential oils in the room, Bergamot and lemongrass. She could make out a sink, a tray with strands of thread or hair, light hair, not dark. Something frilly. A tutu. Janina's. She hadn't worn hers in weeks.

"I think this is my sister's."

"OK, let's go."

They circled around the table past photos clipped to a line. A photo of Bela's window taken from Mrs. Luger's driveway. One with her little sister's face lying in ecstasy in the grass, almost a headshot. How had he done this? She started to run, looking back once at Jane's face, into the oven room—they almost forgot to close the dark-room door—they went upstairs, her nausea imprinted with Janina's face. Her abs were ground beef as she prepared to step out under the sun but they were already at the window with Rick hoisting her on the counter and sliding the glass out. Bela fell to the brick path faster than she could peddle once on an exercise bike and rolled out of the way of Rick coming. He leaned back through the window and swept something off the counter, a fleck of dirt. They slid the window shut. Bela had a premonition and saw shadows pool, someone watching from a window. She seized Rick by the collar, pulled him towards the gate at the end of the yard, refusing to avert her gaze from the exit or recognize the observer's existence. Near the gate they climbed a small slope and the shed's eavestrough eclipsed the sun. Rick tried the gate but it was wire-tied. He kicked it as Bela's phone beeped.

"Let's go out front," he said.

"We can't."

"Climb!" She started up the chain-link gate, which bent floppily, its poles the only sure thing. She flew over the top, landed beside the shed. Rick's khaki leg was caught. He twisted his foot and Bela told him to stop making noise. She pulled on his pants and they ripped as he landed in the lane. They scurried, her heart apelike and bounding towards some unnatural limit. She didn't know who this man was and what he was doing to her—she wanted to tell him to keep going down the lane and leave as they came to her gate beside the parked boat. At the same time she couldn't fully blame him— if she told him to leave she'd have to go to the police on her own, and they already had a file on her for possession.

"What do we do?" she asked.

"Was that your sister in the picture?"

"Yes. And I think that was her dress."

"Does she know him?"

"Are you serious?"

She checked her phone. She'd received an email from a florist, not Jane.

"Let's go inside," she said, regretting she'd ever used a computer.

"All I wanted was to steal something to give to your dad."

"Do we call the police now?"

"I don't know. I don't know if it's a crime to take a picture of a little girl and take her tutu. I mean, what kind of crime."

Bela unlatched the gate and unlocked the side door. She felt like she'd robbed a bank and the sirens would start up, but nothing happened, which only upset her more as she paced back and forth and tried to not look through the window to the Pomeranian's house, where the Oldsmobile was still gone. Jane sat on the rocker, looking hawkeyed out the window.

"Do you know our neighbour? *Ten facet z Pomorza*."

"I don't think," Jane said, looking out.

"You can stop looking."

Bela sat in the dining room and stared at the bearded Aeolus face carved into the handle of a chair. She stared at the crumbs on a saucer. She decided she would avoid eye contact with everyone for the foreseeable future.

"Maybe it's kind of late to go to the police," she said. "I mean, should we go in the morning?"

She leapt up and locked the side door, the back door, the front door. She ran to the front window and closed the curtains, opened them half-way.

"Ron will get his rifle out if we tell him," she said. "He needs to see a doctor. We can't tell him anything that just happened right now."

"Why don't we just skip the concert," Rick said.

"All that's going to happen if we call tonight is they're going to send someone tomorrow, unless we say it's an emergency and tell them everything. We need to get our story straight. What's our reason for being there?"

"Jane, we might need you to watch dad, and dad will watch you," she said as the Oldsmobile pulled into the Pomeranian's driveway.

| Full Pomeranian |

"*And so we're left to assess a thinker who, in exploring the frictional intersections between the phallogocentric Apollonian and the raw wounded jouissance of the Dionysian vagina, cannot stake a claim in explicating these 'personae,' however passionately wrought, as it were, to an intellectual or moral legacy that could offset, if such a thing were permissible, her TERF-adjacent politics, as systematically deconstructed in the previous seminar by my colleague and comrade Kaminska, nor the violence of her remarks about sexual assault. I've tried to be fair in my assessment of her critique of Lacan, Foucault, and the so-called School of Saussure, as well as her recent comments on Maridel Le Sueur and Simone de Beauvoir and her rather welcome championing of Rihanna,*

while not obfuscating displeasure at my subject or decentering our political aims. Thank you."

No one clapped.

Ariel said, "If you have any questions, I'm happy to take them."

"I just want to tell you," Zainub said into the mic, "that your presentation was a step backwards for this community. We need to talk about the way you just offered up an uncritical platform for violent, essentialist ideas."

"No, no, Zainub... no, no." Ariel had no words—could do nothing but shake her head and *no—it isn't like this; know that it's not the way you think it is, that we just need to find the common words.*

"I see you," said Zainub, "I see the way you sat here for a full 20 minutes interrogating all the systems of this 'contrarian thinker'" (in bunny ears), "the way you salted and peppered your presentation with disclaimers and lukewarm denunciations. But I never heard you articulate *why* you were sharing these views, unlike the previous seminar."

She wasn't sure if this was an invitation to speak, and she didn't want to chance anything, but she said: "Zainub, first off, thank y–you for showing up, and for everything you do in this community. I had no intention of presenting these ideas in a disinterested w–way..."

Her voice cracked under the mic 10 metres away, which Zainub pointed at her like a gun.

"Zainub, I'm sorry if I let you down with my presentation. I feel that dissecting these ideas can equip us with the mental technologies we need to understand fascism, to prevent our enemies from gaining a foothold again. That's why I went into such detail about her problematic idea of male creativity, not out of any sympathy. And, if I may, my original topic would have had too much overlap with Comrade Lopez's treatment of—"

"All I'm hearing is post ad hoc rationalizations for platforming hate. Why you would deploy language in any way but to mark out Paglia as a dangerous and unhinged cryptofascist is beyond any understanding, even considering the fact that you're a cis white woman. That's why language is important. For a second there when you quoted her you even started talking like that manic bitch, the way she sounds like she's talking to herself on the toilet. For real, you could have thrown all your slides in the Recycle Bin. You keep saying you're an ally but this is how you marshal your resistance? By taking the kid gloves to this stupid bitch who deserves to be chased off the streets the way they want to chase us down every day?"

Ariel wanted to surrender. She heard the seams of Zainub's Urdu and knew she'd done damage.

"Zainub, I agree with everything you're saying. And I know I need to do better. I appreciate the need for moral rectitude. I want to tell you that I'm resisting every day. I just doxxed this fucking piece of shit my sister's dating. Got someone to take care of him. Trust me, I know I can do better, Zainub, and I thank you for your invaluable perspective and know that I don't mean to speak out of turn of my limited experience. Please know that I'm fighting every day."

She wanted to throw herself at Zainub's feet and kiss them.

"Save me the savior complex. I'll tell you what you don't do. You don't explore Hitler Youth ideas like it's fuckin' Candy Crush. You *do not*! I'm fucking leaving, and I don't care what you say."

Zainub put the mic back in the stand. A few people clapped, maybe at the comment, or the presentation, and then they started leaving the auditorium. Ariel felt like she'd taken a tomahawk to the temple. The grad-school assistant with the room key, some fucking white guy with glasses, stared impatiently. Melissa smiled at Ariel, but then took out her phone and answered a call in a way Ariel found pseudo. Only Beck came over, in her toque, as Ariel trembled like a deer on the side of the road.

"Are you going home?" asked Beck, but she might as well have said nothing, or said it with a five-second delay, because Ariel found herself saying "no…" then "yes…" like words whispered in telephone tag. *Save me the savior complex.*

"What do you mean?"

"Yes."

"Are you OK?"

"Yes," said Ariel. "I mean, I'm going to Bill's to help with, what was it, the canvassing for The Polyculture Sanctuary, or…"

"Can I get a ride?"

"Oh, a ride."

That is why language is important.

"Yes, I can bring you there, I mean, where? I didn't catch that."

Beck stepped closer to Ariel and clasped her forearm. "Home," said Beck. Ariel's arm hair went anti-grav. She stretched her mouth wide three times. She tried to center her focus back on Beck, her old friend: "yes, yes," she said, "thank you." The red-bearded, bespectacled TA was still staring at her, and she felt like a woman in a housecoat stranded in the dunes.

She said, "I was not all there for a second, I was preoccupied."

"I can see that."

They went into the hall and the TA locked the door. The fluorescent lights felt like laughing gas. The song "My Humps" played from an administrative office radio. Ariel grinned psychotically and shivered. *Zainub hates Nazis. She hates me. Therefore, I'm a Nazi? Or she hates more than Nazis?* She bit down on her gums, a babushka of superego over ego liberation unto asymptotic infinity. She laughed in terror.

"Zainub's a bitch," she said.

"What?"

Ariel flexed her mouth muscles like she'd guzzled Robitussin. She said it again: "Zainub's a bitch!"

Sure, she could have given a trigger warning before her PowerPoint. But was she supposed to get Zainub's rubber stamp for all research? If they didn't read bad people, then how would they stake the goalposts, or would they just ban everyone in a cultural revolution—wasn't that puritan zeal more bourgeois than Walmart? but no! this was *wrong*. She needed to take her phone out on the toilet and empty her bladder, writing sentences until her head cleared.

"I need to use the toilet," she said, pushing open the door to the piss-and-Lysol-smelling bathroom. She wrapped the seat and pulled her pants down. She wrote on the Memo app, *I wrote a footnote on Slide 33 that Paglia was "approaching fascism" and how she almost allowed a Nazi to translate her. Do I need to e-mail Zainub this? Why didn't I say this when she was yelling at me? Worked on the PowerPoint for six days in the library. What am I doing? How can I do better? cultural revolution… Am I a Nazi? Motivation?*

a. beaumais

She pulled her pants up, seeing only a drizzle of yellow in the toilet. She flushed it but then she wrapped the lid again and sat down.

She felt like she could piss every drop out and it wouldn't matter. She got up and flushed the toilet and almost sat down again but the voices chirped her and she rammed her head into the metal door. It felt almost good, but she still wanted to piss and so she banged it harder and started forgetting but she wasn't who she needed to be and she started crying till she smashed her head on the coat hook and screamed and the bathroom door opened. She unlatched the stall and Beck ran in and they hugged and she felt disgusting, virus-ridden. She walked to the mirror but there was no blood, only a red goose egg.

"Are you OK?" said Beck.

"Zainub's a bitch!" she screamed.

Beck kept smiling and laughing. Ariel didn't know where this'd come from. It was like she'd smashed a little girl's piggy bank to take the dollar inside.

"Yeah, kind of."

"Am I right? I love her to death."

To gamble everything away before the fun stopped, she screamed into the hall. She was lightheaded enough to forget. She heard nothing but the turnstiles downstairs and she pitied Zainub as a traumatized non-agent. She was profane, her throat raw and tremoring like an ancient cave suddenly entered.

Outside in the parking lot, they got in Ariel's new-car-smelling Kia, Ariel fanning and summoning the smell into her nostrils as though finally admitting she liked the smell of her own farts. Beck laughed. Beck never laughed at anything

Ariel did. Ariel turned the ignition only to slump in her seat: "Is it so much to ask that Zainub would show more civility? I get it. We agree not to talk about Germaine Greer. We oppose white feminism and class reductionist Marxism. We refuse to carry water for Bernie Sanders. We're not going to punch left. But God damn, did it really seem like I was sympathetic?"

"No. Not really. I mean, no."

Ariel could tell that Beck wasn't going to lose sleep over this—over anything. She hated this so much it turned her on. "I love Zainub. She's not afraid of anyone. I know she's a survivor. I mean, more than a Beyoncé song. I'm in no position to pile on, I know what her uncle did to her... But, like, how are we going to work together against the people who share none of our views?"

"I know. I agree with you, Air," with a note of impatience.

Ariel pulled at her hair. She couldn't say it, and she was thankful for the company, but Beck was just a firefly in the Zainubian galaxy inside her brain.

"I admit I'm jealous of Zainub. I've always wanted to curry favour with her."

"Why?" said Beck.

"She never gave a fuck. She's pretty—even if she tries to monetize that. Should I blame her? Her bellybutton in every photo. I don't know. Her band is good. OK, I have a big hard-on for her."

Beck laughed nervously.

"It's just…"

Ariel almost admitted that she couldn't match the potency of Zainub, the way she deconcentrated and milked meaning from her traumas, couch to cafe, seminar to shrink. But the flipside was Zainub's puritan zeal—a zeal that made her not deeper but more *bourgeois* (somehow), and no one in the final telling was deeper than Ariel.

"Like, I'm sorry I'm impure. Sorry that 1% of me had sympathy for Hilary Clinton. Sorry I make my rent payments. Plus her ex. I mean would she have gotten published without that guy? She got a fucking feature in *Slut Scandal* and I got a sidebar. I mean was she better than me? Beck! Answer." She looked with rapey eyes at Beck: "No, no, don't answer. She's smarter than me. OK. Fine. But I see those reply-guys. Her ex would go on stage with a Confederate uniform and do pelvic thrusts as he 'ironically' took it off and burned it. But I'm problematic? You know what, Zainub isn't putting in the work anymore. I'm making a name. She might have more Followers and reply-guys who edit her essays, but when everything is due in the final telling, I feel like she's going to leave behind nothing."

Beck hesitated, watching Ariel's hands on the steering wheel. She nodded: "Yeah. Yeah, it's true, Air."

Ariel was caught in a runaway soak of affirmations and could not help but put her scopes on Beck's chameleon behaviour, her adjustment to whatever temperature.

"Can you please say something besides nodding your head?"

"But I agree with everything you're saying. It's just, I'm not processing everything."

"No, I didn't mean to attack you," said Ariel. "Please don't think that. It's just, I don't even know if you like me, if you believe in anything I say."

"Of course I believe in you! You're one of my favourite girls in the Cell!"

One of.

"But that's exactly what I mean! You keep affirming me. Yes yes you're my yes-woman. How do I know you're serious? How do you do it? You don't seem to have convictions. I mean I'm jealous, but I'm not. I mean, no! I'm fucking stupid!" She plucked a hair out. "Just ignore everything I'm saying. I'm not thinking straight." She looked at Beck. "Please." She tried to hug Beck—she pulled over in a bus lane and unbuckled and reached over to hug her. "Forgive me?"

She squeezed Beck and her tiny leather backpack until Beck patted her shoulder. But the patting was with such hesitation and at such long intervals, like an alien metronome. Ariel stopped hugging. It was like when Shahzad didn't know how to calm her when she was late with one of her papers and had gone against her diet or when she was triggered by something her editor had commented on her essays.

"I'll take you home now," she said.

As she drove, she thought, *Maybe I *am* privileged, maybe I *am* reactionary*. She thought this in a blank, neurotic way, like it was an unfunny joke she wasn't going to acknowledge or contort her face muscles to.

She told Beck, "Maybe I *am* privileged. Maybe I'm a secret fascist."

"Well, most of us are privileged."

"How do you do it," said Ariel. "How do you stay even-keeled. I feel like just having my name out there means waxing my neck for the guillotine. But I'm not going to stop, because it's why I get up in the morning. But I'm tired. I want more instruction. Sometimes I wonder whether my problem is that I'm not very intelligent despite being highly reasonable. Or whether I'm actually really smart but just delusional as fuck. Can you tell me?" She said this slowly and drove sullenly as though pre-emptively puncturing her raft of self-pitying pleasure, because pleasure is a raft that sinks. She didn't want to feel anything except maybe listen to the same song for a few hours and drink wine and get up the balls to edit an essay.

"I'll tell you what I do," said Beck. "If anything interrupts my sleep, then I just stop thinking about it. I go back to how I was before. That's how I know."

"That's terrifying. What if someone dies?"

"I'll allow myself to be sad, but not as long as most people. But yeah, I make exceptions from time to time."

This was as absurd to Ariel as hearing that Beck worshipped the sun, or that living in an authoritarian capitalist state was better because *things got done*. But as she drove and let the idea soak in, she found that it titillated her as much as it appalled her, like some sultry man breathing down her neck and asking if she wanted to be tied up in his hotel room. The idea fracked her; it was clarifying in small doses even if it was wrong.

"I don't know how you can live in that grey state. I mean, doesn't that cheapen your own narrative?" Or maybe, she thought, it was just good social planning. There were people on Reddit she could ask.

She dropped off Beck, watching her turn into a speck in the doorway—one with a half-way meaningful life and a salt-of-the-earth boyfriend. But still, Beck's moderation made her seem, to Ariel, like a Christian Scientist or Lilliputian. Ariel let this new paradigm seep through her, let her cares fork, even if it was not what a good socialist would do. But maybe she was just a socialist so she wouldn't have to address her flaws. So she could just get a new tattoo every time something happened instead of... She did not care anymore.

*

She went to bed early. She tried not to move. Zainub's words were embers under the curtains. The bedroom was hot, but she didn't have it in her to move, and the heat dragged her to deeper chambers of restlessness. It was like someone was shining a flashlight in her eyes but she wasn't sure it would make any difference to close them.

*

She got in the Kia without taking off her Tony the Tiger pajamas. If someone saw her—if she got pulled over, if she got gas—no one would salute her power level, no one would recognize a washed-out Tony the Tiger, and if they did, it'd be taken as proof of her sloth, not of her digging in the crates of mass culture.

She got in a traffic jam on Lake Shore and thought, *Maybe there *are* too many people here, maybe this city isn't the center of the universe.* She was not having an epiphany, but she was talking to herself with something approaching zeal. *I'm tired. I can hardly keep track of the difference between ontology, teleology, and epistemology unless I'm shoving books up my ass all day. I'm still the same person, but I can't clench down all day, I can't breathe everything in, not because I'm unable, not because I can but I'm choosing the lesser path, but because this is the only path left.* She thought for a second that maybe this *was* a lesser path, and the thought of her selfishness, or that she just didn't care, gave her an ASMR-type tickle and hard nipples.

*

a. beaumais

When she pulled in behind the rusty station wagon, she took out her phone, saw that it was 11:30, and decided, instead of entering unannounced, which might both jolt her family and create a precedent (that she couldn't honour) for more frequent appearances, to phone her sister.

Jane picked up within seconds.

"Hi hi."

"Hey," said Ariel. "I'm outside. Are you guys up?"

Mouse-like footsteps through the receiver. Jane opened the door giggling like Ariel was Santa, who'd come to drink the cocoa left out for him. Ariel bent down to hug her. Jane wore a mermaid mask and a long bee-coloured nightgown that felt frozen. Ariel rubbed Jane's back in circles, trying to spark some warmth, but she felt uncomfortable due to the coldness of her sister's body and the fact that she was touching someone in an unsolicited, unconsented way.

"Where's dad?" she finally said. She took off her shoes and Jane traced her hand over the tiger stripes.

"Don't know," she said. "Went somewhere."

"Is he in his room?"

Jane shook her head and followed Ariel upstairs. Ariel did a double-take of the moonlight kindling the yellow nun in the stained glass. She didn't know why she'd come here, besides some clock-like instinct that it was time to peel off a layer of dead skin. They got to Ron's room, the Viking TV playing a true crime show. Ariel remembered the muskiness, the little deposits of pencils and plates and envelopes balanced like Dolmens. She'd inherited the hoarding trait and often blogged about it.

"Ron," she called out. Jane jumped on the bed and picked up her iPad. She was watching a black and white

dox

YouTube video of a nurse ironing a uniform with a red cross. Ariel sat on the edge of the bed and, turning over the two pillows (for reasons of hygiene and propriety), laid her head back among the TV voices. She stared at Jane, who was mouthing words at the iPad over her head. She told Jane to come close, which felt strange to say, for she did not like getting close to children, babies, or animals. Jane nestled into Ariel's shoulder and the two sets of voices crossfired through the room, Jane pulsing heat through Ariel's arm until Ariel fell asleep.

*

pomorskie.txt

Im the doktor
Like a bee in the flowr bocks
Jumping on Pomorskies hed
When he screems in my kimono
Where mamaa gived me lunch
Snifing her, the watermellon
The tayste of her hare, door in tree
The pomorskie screems at me
Kimono wet
His I's no something Bela taykes my hand
No one knows I cannt stop
Where Stasia went?
Why she cant kome taked me to pool?
I swammd in water
She barfed up she left that summer
She stoppd takeding me, screemd
Bela taked off my kimono
She gayve watermellon
Teers ran down legg

a. beaumais

No one new why it cannt stop

Niemiecki boy haff a sister
To dress in Stasias pants
Agata lying beside me
why?
The kimono, the sun
I don't know who shee, her I's
Sister
Ill liy
Ronald gone when he leeved
I ask the fayries in my pillow, in treee, hes
Bringinged mom
And disappeer in mask

*

Ariel opened her eyes, her senses reconstituting under a canvas blanket rough enough to file her corns on. TV static scrambled the room with x-ray arteries pooling over the weather woman giving the forecast. It was 3:58 and there was a crook in the sheets where Jane had lain. Ariel swung her feet around and they hit the ground sooner than expected— her dad had built the bed too low to the ground. What the *actual fuck* if he hadn't come back? She hoped he'd seen them sleeping and had gone to one of the beds downstairs, but something told her this wasn't the case.

She went down feebly in the dark, her compass the spears of moon lapping through the barred window. She forgot where the light switch was in the kitchen, where anyone was, how they'd react to light. She remembered coming up these stairs in grade school, to where her and Bela's bedroom was, when Ron and Stasia slept in the study. The dead years stuck voodoo pins in the present and she dismissed her feeling of nostalgia as brainwashed and bourgeois. She went up to the second floor, to her old bedroom. She inched towards the twin beds and tripped on a chair, her hands grabbing a ledge and almost pushing over a vase. When she found the beds she was scared to touch the duvets because she might have to explain why she was here.

But no one was here.

Ariel went back down to the kitchen and found the light switch. She went to the sunroom and sat on the rocking chair. She didn't have her glasses on, but it looked like Rick's BMW was still outside. She felt a loss of sensation, a ketaminergic doppler effect. Some kind of noise, like muzak or sound effects, dribbled at a low frequency. Ariel stopped breathing and listened, her ears sorting through the sound of a car on the street, the fridge chugging, and this strange new frequency, which came and went and which she attributed to increased activity in her secondary auditory cortex due to upping her Zoloft on the advice of her psychiatrist and Reddit.

She stood, gripping the rocking chair, balance tits-up, TMJ flaring. Maybe she was losing to the voices in her head, but she couldn't stay still. "Jane," she said. Louder. She went to the kitchen and opened the fridge—squinted at the labels of Polish pickle jars. She microwaved two potato pancakes. When the machine dinged, she heard the noise again. She looked through the kitchen window and shuddered. She thought of the possessed little girl in *The Ring*.

"Jane," she said, her hunger burrowing.

"Agata," said a voice in the basement.

She opened the door downstairs upon a melody. There was a television drone, some kind of American anchor voice. The stairs creaked, the humming ceased, the temperature dropped in a crescendo. Wine-cellar chill. Ariel paused at the bottom of the stairs and entered the little room. Jane was kneeled over Ron, pressing her hands into him as blood seeped from his head.

"What are you doing? What happened?"

Jane hummed a song.

Ariel rushed over, almost strangling her sister. "What are you doing?" she cried.

"You must call 911 and get the defibrillator," said the television voice on the iPad.

Jane tilted her father's head back and Ariel told her to stop, but Jane ignored her. She felt her father's body, laid out cold. The blood almost dry, the wrist with the faintest underwater drumming.

Ariel looked at Jane, at Ron's papery blue skin, the curtain call of death. She felt abstracted away from this scene—they'd long been estranged—but this made her tear up more. She caressed Ron's forearm. She put her sweater over his legs. Jane tilted his chin back and squatted over him monkey-like. She breathed into his mouth, mirroring the instructions on the iPad. Ariel wondered if Jane's lungs were strong enough, but Ariel'd stopped powerlifting and was smoking again. Her face was teary and flushed, even as the cellar floor froze her socks. She took out her phone and called 911, panicking she hadn't done so yet, assuring herself that only a minute had passed. "My father's not breathing much," she said into the phone. "We're giving him CPR."

"Do you know what you're doing?"

"Yes, I think." She gave them the address.

"Who are we speaking to? Do you want to stay on

the line?"

"I don't know. I don't know."

She stared at her father, at Jane astride him. She started crying, but she didn't know what to feel. "We're in the basement. I'll unlock the door upstairs."

She hung up and her eyes crossed over her hand holding the phone. Her father had been bad to her. He didn't enunciate his views much, but she knew they beat out from a cold heart of patriarchy. She sobbed as she went upstairs— she knew he'd always wanted her to shut up and make food and babies, grow her hair out and wear sundresses. She knew she was sobbing for herself, not him. *There is no reason to love your parents more than anyone else.* She unlocked the front door, got a glass of water, and fled back downstairs like Reaper in *Overwatch* materializing in a purple cloud, guns ablaze over her father. Jane was on top, pressing his chest, and Ariel cried for him, for herself, for Jane, who could be orphaned any second. How could she stop thinking about herself? Who would take care of Jane? She fell to her father's chest and rubbed it, and he coughed, inhaled, gasped. He sighed and she stopped rubbing, wondered if it was condemning him. "Should we lean him against the wall?" she said. Broken glass everywhere. She swept it with her foot and when her dad started hacking up mucus and opened an eye, she tried to hoist him, but he was too heavy. *It was impossible*, she'd write. Jane pulled his other arm and they slid him closer to the wall. His spit exploded like a wine barrel under a train. Ariel slapped his back, which made him cough harder and she started praying to Vishnu, chanting ohms, louder as he coughed worse. Jane sat between his legs and hugged him as he coughed in her face and she took it like a blessing. His body started shaking and Jane covered him in tears. Jane said something in Polish in his ear, something Ariel couldn't understand, about their mother, or maybe his middle name. Ariel's sweat ran hot over Jane and her father, dripping on his pantleg. She said goodbye to him and wished she could go instead, remembered him bringing her to the first day of school, the front lawn, the children lined up in their dresses and Sunday best, one boy telling fart jokes, and she decided to do something crazy the moment her father stopped breathing. Jane was right there, the smelly little girl, and she hugged them both as she heard the door upstairs, which she'd forgotten, and voices spilled through, and she'd never leave here, would never let go as she felt her father cough louder as she kissed him on the cheek and he struggled to open his eyes like they were beggars in a storm, and the footsteps became hands gripping her and the lights twinkled like Christmas and men came and pushed Ariel to the wall and two men and a woman heaved her father onto a long rectangle of cloth that Ariel's eye interpreted as a stretcher. Jane started screaming in Polish and flailing her arms, the woman pulling an oxygen mask over Ron's face, and Ariel stepped forward with her hand, "he's choking," stepping in glass so her sock ran red, walking forward as the medics laid him on the stretcher and pressed his chest and he coughed and barfed, Jane screaming *Krzysztof* until at last he swallowed and swallowed again. They gave him water and he wanted more, they started giving it to him and he stole the bottle, pacing the room, glass crinkling underfoot as Jane lunged at him and he picked her up. The medics took Jane away. They told Ron to sit on the stretcher and he saw Ariel and pointed at her with the same expression as on the night she graduated high school. She told him in Polish to sit on the stretcher—that he was sick—and he listened to her. For a moment, everything was silent except for YouTube. Ariel had space-ship tinnitus as a man's words—*Please, cooperate with us, do you understand me*—got caught in the net of her senses. There was no room for all of them. She took her father's arm as he got off the stretcher and wandered like he'd been disturbed in his sleep by a thief on the front lawn. The medics followed like dog catchers and Ariel took his hand slowly up the stairs. Ron's fingers were icicles and he paced the kitchen, reaching for a banana on the counter. One of the medics tried to take it from him but recanted. "So what we're going to do," said the woman medic, with conductor-like hand gestures and astronomically enunciated syllables, like she was the Madonna talking to a cargo bay of trafficked humans, "is we're going to recommend that your father come in for an ECG," pointing to her chest and making a heart-thumping motion with her fist. "Does that sound good? Does your father speak English?"

Jane yelled something in Polish that Ariel couldn't understand and the female medic put her hand up.

"He speaks English when he wants to," said Ariel.

The female medic stepped up to Ariel and centered her world on her.

"You can take him in," said Ariel, wanting everyone to turn away from her pimples.

"Ron... *Tato*."

Ariel couldn't believe how beautiful the woman was, her pointy nose and greying hair, a lost aunt whose house she could sleep at and discuss her love life and essays. Her feet thawed on the kitchen tiles. She wanted to grab the woman and kiss her. All she had to do was put one foot in front of the next. "Ron, *idź z tą miłą panią*."

a. beaumais

"Do you want to come with or stay here?" said the woman.

Ariel looked at Jane and at her tiger-stripe PJs and red sock. She felt like she'd dunked her head in a frozen pond.

"You can stay," said a medic. "You look tired."

"Yes, yes," Ariel said, and soon after she confirmed her phone number they were gone, the male medics having led Ron out as the beautiful female caressed his shoulder on the stretcher like he was a suicide risk.

Jane yelled for Stasia.

Ariel went upstairs and Jane followed. They held hands, stopped on the second-floor landing to look at each other. Ariel thought she should have gone with her father.

"Do you think we should go to the hospital?"

"I want sleep. I was thinking about Fred."

This affirmation of Ariel's decision not to go only gave her more doubt, in line with her psychological profile. But as she floated up to her father's bed, she did not think she could operate a vehicle or talk her way through the frontlines of a front desk.

She wanted to ask who Fred was, but already Jane was making extraterrestrial sleep noises in bed as she tunnelled under Ariel's arm. Ariel stared at the ceiling. She was unmoored, her inner voices lapping at her like flames that burnt out as soon as they made contact. She was thankful for the feeling of release, even at the cost of her father's health. (*I knew he'd be OK*, she would write.) She felt, for a second, that nature had a way of imposing order, like a medieval mob taking a battering ram to her castle wall, that her nagging unsleeping idealism was getting dungeonraped by time— this was against her moral code and she gave her super ego the floor to draw a distinction between BDSM as fetish and patriarchal violence as a symbol of order. Yet she felt that maybe she would be forced to change, the way the setting sun acts as a bookmark even on violently schitzed-out days.

She spooned Jane, telling herself she'd go to the hospital in a few minutes once this bowling ball of anxious gravity slid off, but she lapsed beneath the waves into repetitive bizarro ruminations about gingerbread houses and TA office hours, which fell through a trap door into a cozy strawbedded blackout cocoon with Jane. Her breath slowed like a train coming to the station in timespace, hurtling at a snail's pace in the clouds, a comet through an eye-bleeding Fijian archipelago, the walls of the comet rumbling and shaking and pounded on by an angry landlord, and Ariel flickered awake in her father's bed, staring at herself from the ceiling, the rapping continuing—a crunching noise on a familiar pane of wood. She opened her eyes at the next bang, squeezing her sister and her bedsheet to test consciousness like putting a foot on the ground when drunk. Jane mumbled something, did not disappear, so Ariel assumed she was not dreaming. But the knocking on the door? She hadn't lived here for years and doubted her mind was capable of something so fastidious as remembering that sound, if she was honest. She heard the knocking again. She sat up in bed. She opened the curtain upon a white van parked on the street by a sycamore, maybe too small to be an ambulance. What would the medics want? She turned back and Jane was awake, standing there. They went down the steps to the front door, which vibrated with knocking. Ariel wiped the rheum from her eye and opened the door. It was the Pomeranian. His face was beet-red and his hairy, meaty fist quivered like a dying centipede.

"I'm sorry! Can I help you?"

"Who was in my house?"

"Excuse me?"

"Which one?"

"Oh shit, the paramedics came to your house? My dad is sick. Sorry they disturbed you."

"What are you saying?" he said, and Ariel felt the same way, and with higher ground to stand on, seeing as how he'd knocked on their door at 5 a.m. But she was still suffering some goodwill, so she inhaled and said, "About that thing with the lawn, don't worry. I just think we should drop that. How does that sound?"

She expected him and his whispering neck veins to push off back to his lair.

"Someone broke into my house."

"Did you call the police?"

"Was your sister. I swear by it."

"Jane?" Ariel turned and saw her peeking through her mermaid mask behind the kitchen door. "Couldn't have been."

The Pomeranian smiled. "Your *OTHER* sister."

It felt perverse to hear his knowledge of her family.

"She's not home tonight. I really don't think–"

"Bring your sister. Get her."

"Um, no. We'll sort this out in the morning. What time is it? I told you, my dad's sick and–"

He pushed past her into the house. His flyswatter hand slammed the door shut.

"What the hell are you doing? I did not invite you in. Get *out!* NOW!"

"Call the police then," he said, shifting on his feet. His eyes capped a nervous energy multiplying like a tropical ant colony.

"I will, and they'll come right away."

The nightmare spun like a top in the garden of her fatigue.

"Do it."

Her dreaminess was shredded by pinpricks, her line of sight narrowing in high-def on the Pomeranian's whiskers and cherry wizened pores. She turned her head part-way but did not want to look at Jane and add her to the equation. She glanced at her phone and back at the Pomeranian, visualizing the 911 finger-motion.

"I don't know–," she was saying, when there was a knock at the door.

The Pomeranian held up his hand. He grabbed the knob and started to open, paused, then opened it fully.

It was Rick. Like a Chernobyl to her rescue.

"Where's my sister?" Ariel asked.

"I don't know."

"I'm serious."

Rick looked at the Pomeranian and swallowed.

He said to Ariel: "I came as fast as I could when you texted me."

"My dad's at the hospital and now..."

Rick looked again at the Pomeranian, about to flee.

Ariel: "Did you and Bela do something?"

Rick shuddered, stepping back: "Well, no, but…"

"Did Bela do something?"

The Pomeranian pulled Rick inside and slammed the door.

"I'm sorry! It was the stupidest thing, we wanted to talk to you and we tried to see if you were there–"

a. beaumais

The Pomeranian clutched Rick's neck like a chicken's and Rick grabbed the hand but it tore down his shirt and buttons pinged on the floor. Rick looked ghosteyed at Ariel. She didn't care if they killed each other as long as they left.

"What do you want?" shouted Rick. "What do you want?"

The Pomeranian kneed him in the stomach and Rick collapsed. "Take this outside," she said, moving closer, the Pomeranian's knee docked in Rick's gut as he straddled him like a sacrificial goat. "Do you want me to call the police?"

"Yes, let's t–tell the police what I did," said Rick on the hardwood.

The Pomeranian jammed his other boot into Rick's knee and Ariel heard bones crack.

"Stop it. I can p–pay you a–a–a–lot." He was crying.

The Pomeranian coughed hard, collecting mucus. "Godforsaken devils!"

Ariel said, "He probably has more in common with you than you think."

"What?" said Rick. "I came to help your d–"

"Shut your hole," said the Pomeranian, pinning him harder.

Ariel saw something black under the Pomeranian's shirt and she reached for her phone.

Jane screamed in the kitchen. The Pomeranian looked at Ariel.

"Give me your phones," said the Pomeranian.

"Why?"

"I'm putting down this devil."

Ariel put her iPhone on the counter as Rick twisted his elbow back. He was half the Pomeranian's weight but sixty times as helpless—she almost pitied him. Rick's struggle session kicked up Bela's "ADDICT" spray as Jane wailed like a baby.

"Make her shut up!" shouted the Pomeranian.

"Jane," she called, but couldn't match the volume.

Ariel hoped the Pomeranian wouldn't touch her—like an off-label privilege of patriarchy. Her thumb twitched with the muscle memory of opening the dictation app where she started blog posts. *Is there any fundamental difference between these two men?* she wondered, breathing in the violence in her childhood home. She felt that maybe the dox was too much, that Rick was bleeding from the mouth and maybe it counted for something against things he'd written on the Internet.

"You guys need to leave," she said.

"Let me go," croaked Rick.

The Pomeranian started death-gripping Rick's neck. Rick struggled and turned mushroom blue and cried out, "I saw what you hid down there, I saw your basement! Pictures of Ja—"

The Pomeranian bellowed in his gut and pulled out a gun from under his shirt.

Rick started bawling and the Pomeranian was too and Ariel darted to the living room. She recognized the toy-like ridges of the Glock 19 from her self-defense class. She shook, the men's cries licking the curtain of what her ears were meant to hear.

Jane hid behind the Christmas tree they never took down. A puddle diffused under the pickle ornament. The tree shook and Jane's teeth chattered. Ariel squeezed her and covered her eyes and the Pomeranian yelled, "Come or I'll shoot!"

a. beaumais

Ariel started back to them. She could not get enough air. If he shot Rick, maybe he'd shoot her. When she turned the corner the Pomeranian was flushed pink like a hot dog. She stood in the doorway, flinching with the Glock's movements mirroring the Pomeranian's breath.

"Bela knows what she saw," said Rick. "Are you going to kill everyone? She saw!"

"Fuck you!" said Ariel. "I did *not* invite any of you into my life! I did *not* ask for this!"

"What's your mother's name," the Pomeranian asked.

"My–? Stasia. Anastazja."

She could hear whimpers from the Christmas tree. Jane started gaining volume in a shrill spire and Ariel tried to breathe and said in Polish: "Go out the back door and call the police. Make sure Bela doesn't come inside."

She heard a little rustling of ornaments and the Pomeranian turned back with his pistol. Her heart pinched. She hoped he was Czech or Austrian and not Polish.

"*Wierzę w Boga, Ojca Wszechmogącego Stworzyciela nieba i ziemi,*" she said, palms together.

Rick started bawling and tried to stop, his shudders adding a reverb, tears flooding the hardwood. "I'm s–sorry. I promise if you spare us, we won't say anything. We will never speak about what w–we saw."

Ariel: "What did you see?"

The Pomeranian pressed his boot harder into Rick's neck.

"If you kill us, you better k–kill yourself," Rick shouted, "because Bela saw everything. The only path forward is you leave and we never speak of this again. If anyone does, you can find me and bring your gun. My name is Rick Speer,

dox

I live on Lake Shore at 22–"

"Open your mouth!" The Pomeranian bootfucked Rick in the knee and shoved the pistol between his teeth. Rick's gums bled and Ariel looked away and tried to do a box pattern with her breathing, four in, four hold, four out, four hold, four in, four hold, four out.

"Do you have a mother?"

Rick started choking and Ariel felt a pang of black sorrow for him, a beautiful rotted petal buried in her own black silica. She wanted to scream, to run, to intervene in the building blocks tumbling before her, but she closed her eyes and all she could hear was teeth dancing on the gun. Then the unlatching safety, and she smelled coffee in the kitchen on the first day of grade one and remembered her dad in a ski mask and wondered if she'd ever see anyone again.

"Don't do this," she whispered. "Just leave. I don't know what happened but don't do this."

When there was no response, she added, "You know where we live."

Ariel imagined a siren in her head, but it got louder, shriller, and she opened her eyes as the Pomeranian stuck the gun deeper in Rick's mouth till he vomited a black lullaby on himself and started gagging and Ariel imagined taking a carving knife from the kitchen but the Pomeranian took the gun from Rick's mouth, took his foot off, and bounded out the door, slamming it so hard the stained glass over the stairs rattled.

Rick leapt up and put one hand to his stomach, ran his tongue along his bloody teeth. Ariel followed him to the sink, where he filled his mouth and spat out a hot-pink stream. She was not sure whether to help him. What had he done with Bela? She went to the foyer to lock the door, the siren echoing as she remembered Jane. She wanted to go out the back patio to find her, but she saw someone through the window—a ponytailed police officer.

She opened the door for the officer, whose bony arms tensed towards the holster.

"Hello officer," materialized Rick.

The cop looked at him and at Ariel, putting the logical two and two together.

"What's going on? Whose house is this?"

"It's her fa—"

"She can speak for herself!" said the officer. She looked at Ariel. "Are you here because you want to be?"

Ariel was conflicted. "Yes, this is my father's house."

"We got a call from a little girl who gave her name as Janina. We didn't understand what she was saying. Where is she?"

"I'm not sure—she might be out front."

They stepped down from the stoop, Ariel waiting to get shot in the face. The officer kept looking at her and she wondered whether to explain what happened. The officer stared and Ariel yelled to Rick, "Get out there and look for her!"

The officer gave her a double take. "What's going on?"

"My father had a heart attack. I mean, we're upset."

"Your sister was saying something about your mother."

"Yes." She almost teared up but the tongue of her consciousness was scrubbed clean. "She's autistic."

Rick ran towards the ravine calling Jane's name, parting bushes, angling his body away from the Pomeranian's house. Ariel went down the walkway with the officer, hesitating.

"Are you okay?"

dox

Rick was crouched near a duck pond. Ariel could hear a little-girl voice in a freefall of sobs. "Come here," he was saying.

Ariel and the officer got to a rosebush where Jane was dripping in her mermaid mask like she'd run through the pond, her tears and ashen hair raining on the grass.

"Do you want to come out for us?" the officer said.

Jane shook her head. She said something in Polish that Ariel couldn't understand.

High-beams shot down the street and a Honda Civic with an earpiece-wearing driver pulled up, braking before the police car. Bela stepped out. She started towards the house and Jane rolled over like a mud gnome and ran past everyone shouting. She yelled for Bela and jumped up into her arms, fingerprinting her neck with mud.

"What happened?" Bela asked.

Ariel didn't know what to say—it wasn't her fashion not to broadcast. She had so much to tell her, but she knew nothing she said could faze Bela. Maybe she'd stop telling everyone everything all the time.

"Dad had a heart attack," she said.

"What?"

"He's at the hospital. I think he's going to be OK."

"We're all going to be OK," said Rick, and everyone ignored him.

"This is all my fault," said Bela. "Are we going there now?"

"I can drive," said Rick.

"No. I mean, we can go soon." Ariel turned to the officer: "Thank you for coming. I'm sorry to waste your time. We're going to go see our dad."

"What happened? Someone tell me," Bela said.

"Dad had a fall, I think. Jane found him and rev–. Jane found him."

"Thank you, officer," said Bela, and the officer smiled at her.

Ariel noted the superior reception Bela got simply on the power of lookism.

The officer complimented Jane's mermaid mask and went back to her cruiser as Ariel shepherded everyone to the house like they were her kids. She wondered if she'd be forced to accept Rick, to call off the dox, to accept him—when her family had never accepted Protestants or atheists—but Bela was ignoring him, which was welcome to her.

When they got inside, Ariel locked the door and brought everyone to the basement.

"Bela, the Pomeranian barged through the door and almost killed your boyfriend. And now you can tell me what the fuck you guys did."

Bela put a hand to her forehead and exhaled. "He's not m–"

"I'll drive you guys to the hospital and find you a hotel," said Rick.

"What was in his basement?" Ariel asked.

"What the hell happened in *this* basement?" Rick stared at the blood. "He could have killed us both. But it's mutually assured destruction. Just lay low for a few days and I'll try to reach out to him. He almost shot me," said Rick through swollen, Botox-like lips. "I don't know if we should tell the police."

No one said anything and Rick said, "We're gonna make it, fam."

dox

Bela let out a silent scream. Ariel imagined the Pomeranian pulling the trigger. Would she be dead too? She liked the idea of finding solutions outside the criminal justice system, but not with Rick as savior. Maybe she'd have to call off the dox until her family was safe. But if Bela didn't like him anymore, then maybe he'd take himself out of the picture. These things had a way of sorting themselves out.

Jane ran to Rick and wrapped herself around his leg. He patted her like a patriarch and she cooed and squealed. Tears ran under her mask and she muttered something babyish and nonsensical and Ariel wondered, problematically, if Jane needed a dose of Strattera to regulate her, but Bela was nonplussed, her mouth gaping like she wanted to enjoy the silence.

"*Gdzie jest moja matka?*" Jane asked Rick.

"What's she saying?"

"She's asking if you know where our mother went," said Bela.

"No, but I feel like I'll find her soon."